A SEASON AT THE GRAND

ROMANCE AT THE GILDED AGE RESORTS
BOOK THREE

SHERRI WILSON JOHNSON

WILD HEART
BOOKS

Cover design by Evelyne Labelle at Carpe Librum Book Design. www.carpelibrumbookdesign.com

ISBN-13: 978-1-942265-75-7

To my daughter, Kayla
Your world opened up the moment your hands first cupped a digital camera. You've carved out your path in this world as a photographer, never fearing traveling the globe to capture just the right image. You've proven to yourself how strong you are, and to many that when God gifts someone with talents, He helps them use them for His glory. May you always remember the Gifter and hold to your roots no matter where your dreams take you. May your success continue and adventures never cease.

Behold the fowls of the air: for they sow not, neither do they reap, nor gather into barns; yet your Heavenly Father feedeth them. Are you not much better than they?

— MATTHEW 6:26

CHAPTER 1

 oint Clear, Alabama
1905

Amelia Harris stepped off the *Baldwin* with one gloved hand in the porter's hand and the other gripping the handle of her camera case. She could not afford for either of them to land in Mobile Bay. If she lost her camera, then her summer in Point Clear would end before it began, also terminating her career with *The Photographic Times.* They had sent her here to capture nature photographs as well as images of the elite guests enjoying their seaside holiday, and she couldn't allow any mishaps to derail her assignment.

Besides, the summer here enjoying the same luxuries of the wealthy meant a reprieve from the matchmaking of Aunt Polly and Aunt Patsy. Why did they insist her marriageable years had an expiration date and that her occupation as a photographer would damage not only her reputation but her future, as well? Why did they think a woman only twenty-five years old couldn't still find a husband?

"Miss?" The porter's voice snapped her out of her rumination.

With a quick nod and a prayer her embarrassment hadn't touched her cheeks more than the June heat already had, she smiled, then released his hand. "Thank you, sir."

"My pleasure. Enjoy your stay at the Grand Hotel. Your belongings will arrive in your room shortly."

Amelia smoothed her left hand across her stomach and breathed a sigh. As though that would calm the butterflies which flooded inside her. What did she have to be anxious about? While this might be her first assignment this far from home and without a chaperone or colleague, she carried herself well among the elite and had nothing to fear. Besides, she was here to photograph, not to make friends. Her presence as a commissioned photographer required no further burden of proof.

With *The Photographic Times* expecting a minimum of two thousand nature images for their penny post-cards, socializing sat at the bottom of her priority stack. Best she decide right now to pack her jitters away in her trunk along with her swimwear and leave them there all summer.

Pressing her shoulders against the coastal humidity,

she took a step down the boardwalk toward her awaiting adventure.

"Jimmy, come back here. No running on the boardwalk, young man," a woman's stern voice called from behind Amelia.

Before she could peek over her shoulder for a hint at the commotion, a boy—Jimmy, most likely—broke through the cluster of guests and slammed into her, ripping her case from her hand.

"Oh no!" She fell to her knees on the weathered boardwalk and grasped the case seconds before it spun its way into the glistening bay. With her hat now dangling by its string across her back and her body splayed out on top of the leather case like a dead fish, she must already be the subject of the onlookers' gossip. Surely, it would be better if she reboarded the bay boat and returned to Philadelphia this instant.

"Miss, are you all right?" As a deep voice floated over her, heavy with obvious concern, she pushed off the case and attempted to stand.

But her shoe had entangled itself in the hem of her skirt, and she wasn't going anywhere without this gentleman's assistance.

"Here, allow me." He extended his hand to her.

With no choice, she placed her hand in his while raising her chin as she sucked in her embarrassment.

He helped her to her feet, her grasp on the case handle tighter than before.

When her gaze met his, she gulped.

Titus Overton? The general manager of the resort and one of the most eligible bachelors of the South held her hand. Of course, she would sprawl out in front of someone of his status.

He pointed his glassy stare at her, then smiled without showing his teeth, which would have been a difficult task with such a thick mustache resting on his upper lip. The portraits she'd seen of him in the society section of the newspaper hadn't revealed the blueness of his eyes, how even the waters of the Gulf of Mexico were no match for them. Nor had those images hinted at the sandiness of his hair. Indeed, it was as if he were made from the very nature that surrounded him.

Her belly did another flutter, which raced upward and took her heart prisoner.

No, no, no, you are here to work. Nothing else.

"Miss..."

She cleared her throat. "Yes, Miss Harris, Amelia Harris. I'm here with *The Photographic Times* by way of Philadelphia."

He nodded and released her hand. "Of course, well, if you are satisfactory now, stable on your feet, I'll let you proceed to the registration desk."

"Yes, yes, of course. I—well—there was a boy who pushed past me and ripped my camera case from my hand. I assure you, I am not a clumsy woman by nature."

"Under the circumstances, especially after being aboard a vessel for so long, I'd say you handled yourself quite gracefully. A lesser woman would have gone over the edge." He smiled again, little crinkles surrounding the outer corners of his eyes. "Titus Overton, general manager. Pleased to make your acquaintance. I'm certain we will see each other again. Do not hesitate to ask me if you need assistance with anything regarding your photography."

With cheeks ablaze and threatening to set her entire being afire, she gave another nod, then returned her hat to her head. Putting one foot in front of the other and steering clear of the edge, she marched away from what counted as her most humiliating experience to date.

Lord, please don't let this be an indication of how this summer will go. I need this assignment and the time away from home.

~

M iss Amelia Harris. From Philadelphia.

Titus watched her walk away, hands inside his suitcoat pockets, the warmth of her gloved hand still tingling on his.

Was it the heat that sucked every bit of moisture from his mouth and throat, or was it the flaxen-haired woman with the appropriate amount of pink gracing her cheeks? With eyes like sapphires in the most perfect almond shape, she could rule the entire world. If he guessed right about her, she had no clue about the lasting impression a first interaction with her made.

Titus swallowed—or at least tried to—as the traveling photographer disappeared into the main building. Would her accommodations be suitable enough for such a fine and lovely woman? For if she requested something different, something with a view of the bay, he'd make it happen. As manager of the resort, he could do that.

As the last of his forty new guests exited the boardwalk and followed the crushed-shell path to the hotel, Titus pivoted toward the bay and released his breath. The pelican on the post at the end had the right idea.

Freedom.

Landing wherever the wind took him.

Nothing tethering him to anything or anyone except his need for food.

Removing his hat, he retrieved his kerchief from his pocket, then wiped the sweat from his brow and the back of his neck. The summer's heat was only beginning. The start of the almost-endless noise from guests who would come and go throughout the season meant little peace for Titus. Little privacy. Scarce thinking time. No time for planning his future far away from the resort.

One day, he'd shed the obligations that came with managing the Grand Hotel, obligations Uncle Sidney had placed on him when Cousin Norman drowned at sea. Uncle Sidney's position on the board of directors and his greed assured his wishes came true. This time, at Titus's expense. Uncle Sidney had been so good to him during his formative years, but after losing Norman, he'd placed all the expectations he'd had of his son on Titus's shoulders. One day wouldn't be here soon enough.

After returning his hat to his head, he shoved his hands into his suitcoat pockets again with a sigh. If Titus didn't mind himself, this summer might also mean the end of his carefree days as an unattached man, if previous summers were any indication of the matchmaking that transpired when wealthy women took their holidays.

He'd vowed after losing Evelyn he'd never let his heart betray him again, never let his gaze admire a woman for more than a few moments. Just enough to give his heart that little lift of glee it needed every so often. That tingle that reminded him of love's purpose.

But then it had to stop there.

The *Baldwin* sputtered away from the boardwalk, and the last of his staff wheeled carts of trunks and luggage toward the hotel, leaving him alone with the pelican and his thoughts. Alone, that was, until the warm gulf breeze whipped across him, sending the pelican into the air and making Titus wish he could fly away with him.

His migratory bird research and his efforts to protect them, watching the males and females find their mates, build their nests, then start their families—was all he needed. Not the noise humans brought with them, not the heartbreak that accompanied entanglements.

Straightening his shoulders, he nodded to no one but himself and strengthened his resolve. His mission involved getting through this summer while searching for a replacement, then moving on to the work he really wanted to do—preserving nature and doing something that mattered. Unencumbered by a mate of his own. Free and limitless like the gulls and the pelicans.

No Miss Amelia Harris from Philadelphia would hinder his objectives. No, sir, she would not.

~

*A*melia didn't mind that her room didn't face the bay, nor did she mind the simplicity of its furnishings. She'd spend most of her time outdoors photographing, anyway. As long as the bed brought support and comfort at the end of each day and didn't squeak or creak too much, she couldn't ask for more. Facing east, it would provide her with the rising sun each morning streaming through the window, which was all she needed for her prayer and Scripture time.

She might even take advantage of the seats beneath the moss-draped oaks twenty feet outside her door for her time with the Lord. She had much to thank Him for. First, over all, her safe travels and the unscathed equipment. Given the multiple trains she'd boarded plus the steamboat from Mobile to Point

Clear, it had taken miracles to keep everything in good condition.

All her trunks now sat at the foot of her bed except for the trunk with her developing chemicals. Due to their toxic and flammable nature, she didn't want them with her. Plus, the management had insisted they be kept in one of the outbuildings until she needed them for her darkroom. Since most of her film wouldn't be developed until she returned home, she'd only need the darkroom for developing the photographs of the resort per the magazine's agreement with the owner. She'd photograph the management and staff, the guests enjoying the festivities at the resort, and schedule appointments with the guests for family portraits. Officially, she'd work three hours a day except on Sundays and had the freedom to take additional photographs at her leisure.

With her work not beginning until Monday, she could enjoy tonight's dinner and dancing plus the service in the morning. Surely, the resort provided a minister for the guests.

Amelia laced her shoes, wiping a smudge from the brown leather toe of her left shoe, then stood from the bed and focused on her reflection in the mirror. She'd sent her black skirt to the laundry for cleaning after her collision with the boardwalk.

Tonight, her lilac chiffon dress with pink roses embroidered down the front had its chance to shine. The lace sleeves, which came to her elbows and boasted pink ribbons tied in bows, added an extra dose of gaiety to Amelia's heart. Aunt Patsy had insisted she bring the dress for dancing. Although she had no intention of dancing with anyone tonight or any night this summer, there was no harm in looking her best. Once guests found out she had come to take photographs of their families on holiday, they would expect someone who looked friendly, well-kempt, and professional all at the same time. So tonight, she'd make a favorable impression on as many as she could and hope her appointments filled up, leaving no gaps in her schedule.

A smile touched her lips as her eyes drew tight in a smile of their own. Would it be completely terrible if she danced tonight? Just one dance? She hadn't done so since the winter gala, and the only gentlemen who'd asked for her company on the dance floor were ones her aunts had pushed toward her. No one had awakened her heart, and since none had come calling, she must not have stirred any curiosity in them either.

Giving a twist to the left, then to the right, Amelia checked her reflection again. While she wasn't the most beautiful woman in the world, she had features men had complimented in the past. But to capture more than momentary attention from the gentlemen at the Grand, she needed more than a handsome appearance. She needed wealth and a desire to fill a home with children. She had neither. Mama and Pa hadn't left her with much when they passed, and her aunts weren't among Philadelphia's most elite. Given her chosen path of traveling for photography, she'd placed herself in an awkward position—one that very well could turn her into a spinster, as her aunts feared.

She shrugged.

No matter. None of that mattered this summer. Nor did it matter if she danced with any gentlemen tonight. She'd keep her expectations low because she'd most assuredly fail to meet the expectations of any of the gentlemen here at the Grand.

On her way out the door, she snatched her new Kodak Brownie camera. Perhaps if she found herself lacking in conversation, she could fill her time with capturing some of the evening's gaiety. And perhaps a stroll to the boardwalk could offer an opportunity to capture the sunset over the western horizon. A tingle jolted to her toes merely thinking about capturing a pelican in flight or a dolphin emerging from the sea. The evening held endless possibilities she could enjoy and whispered reminders of the promising days ahead.

CHAPTER 2

*T*itus made his way to each of the linen-covered tables, adorned with the finest hand-painted china from London. Plates boasted lobster and salmon, heavy sauces, scalloped potatoes, and steamed vegetables. While guests indulged in the savory delights, he circulated amongst them and played the part he'd been assigned. As Uncle Sidney constantly reminded him, patrons with money and connections would only return and refer their friends if they were satisfied with their experience at the Grand. Ensuring they knew he was here for whatever they might need was a vital part of their satisfaction.

So he smiled, shook hands, listened to complaints. Whatever he must do to guarantee they stayed their entire reserved stay and returned next year, he would do it. Except court their daughters.

Thankfully, he'd already prepared his speech for

when a tycoon or his wife tried to match him with their daughter or niece. It would be unfair of him to spend more time with one woman than he spent with another. Showing any preference could cause hurt feelings, and that was bad for business.

That's what he would tell any of the guests who might propose such a thing. And if it didn't work, he'd let them in on his plans for the future—giving up his position here for a spot on the new Audubon society's team documenting migratory birds. No father would want to match his daughter with a man who couldn't promise a future of stability.

Dr. Joe Alexander from St. Louis and his wife—was it Mary?—had tried to match him with their daughter Constance last summer. Not only had she been allergic to birds, which could never work in a woman's favor where he was concerned, but she'd been three inches taller than him and four years his senior. Besides the fact that his heart had not healed from Evelyn's death after her bout with malaria, at twenty-six, he couldn't bring himself to court a woman approaching her third decade before he approached his own.

Lieutenant Joseph Sanders had tried to pair him with his widowed niece, Lavinia Baker from Virginia, over Christmas when he'd been there with the local Audubon Society trying to bring awareness to the massacre of thousands of birds for the sake of the millinery trade. Not only was he more interested at the time in saving the egrets and herons at Virginia Beach, but Lavinia had five children including a set of twins, and it took every ounce of couth Titus could muster to decline the opportunity with cordiality. What had the man been thinking? Wouldn't he want a man who planned to relocate to Virginia where Ms. Baker had already established her home? Uprooting all those children wouldn't be wise. Besides, Titus wanted freedom, not the encumberment that came with an instant family.

Titus strode to the last row of tables while shaking his head over the preposterousness of the lieutenant's proposition.

If he ever decided to marry—a big *if*—it would be to a woman of his own choosing and not to someone where the arrangement made sense to someone else and not to him.

As he approached the table where the Bishop family from Milwaukee sat, he gave a nod to Charles Bishop, then a wave toward his Mrs.

Judith? Meredith? Oh, what is her name?

Titus accepted his hand and gave it a firm pump, trying to ignore the melted butter Charles had transferred to him by way of the handshake. "Mr. Bishop, wonderful seeing you again this year, and your family. I trust your accommodations are to your liking?" He slid his hand into his pocket and wiped the butter onto his kerchief. Good thing he'd switched it to his dinner suit.

"Oh yes, everything is satisfactory. Edith remarked

how close our quarters are to the pinochle lounge, so she will remain quite occupied this summer."

Edith. That was her name.

Titus smiled and gave her a nod. "Very pleased to hear you're all satisfied."

Charles scratched his chin and gave a quick side glance at his daughters. "Effie and Ettie are starting finishing school in the fall, and then they'll receive courters. We're confident by next spring they'll both have offers of marriage."

Both young women giggled behind their hands while batting their eyelashes at him.

Did Charles and Edith see the sweat Titus felt on his forehead? If so, did they mistake it for the common jitters a gentleman might experience while working up the courage to ask a woman to dance or to take a stroll on the path in front of the bay? If so, they were greatly mistaken, and it was time for Titus to activate his exit plan.

Clearing his throat, he focused his gaze on Charles. "How exciting for your daughters and for your entire family. I do hope next summer when you return, your party will have two new sons by marriage included." He dipped his chin at Mrs. Bishop, then the daughters. "Have a fine stay at the Grand."

Before anyone else captured him in another grueling, uncomfortable exchange, Titus pivoted toward the kitchen and wouldn't stop until he'd exited into the private courtyard for the staff. How would he survive three months of conversations that always seem to be laced with ulterior motives? Maybe he should turn in his resignation tonight, hop on the next bay boat, and escape to Daphne or go up the Mississippi River or over to New Orleans. Anything would be better than this.

When something in the shadows along the wall danced into his peripheral, Titus halted and swiveled in that direction. His gaze landed on Miss Harris, dressed in a pale violet-colored gown, gloves up to her elbows, and hands folded in front of her—and that's when his knees went weak. What was it about this woman that her presence alerted him even in a room filled with women dressed in the same or better fashion? Whatever it was, he had to resist it.

But when she waved and smiled, his feet betrayed him and led him straight to her.

~

*W*hether or not the photographs would develop well due to the dimness in the room despite the gas lighting, Amelia couldn't know. But she pressed the button on her Kodak Brownie, anyway. The elaborately adorned tables surrounded by guests dressed in the latest fashions straight out of *Woman's Day* begged to be captured. While her memory would hold tight to this night for years to come, she prayed at least one of the photographs captured this scene.

As she peered through the lens to find one more perfect angle, the viewfinder filled with Titus Overton coming straight for her. She pressed the button, sealing his image into the next available slot on her roll of film. Then she pressed again. While the images most likely would blur due to his motion, maybe she'd captured his face, at least.

As he drew closer, her heartbeat quickened. Lowering the Brownie, she studied his expression. The intensity gave her alarm. Was he angry she'd been photographing during dinner? That she'd photographed him? He couldn't have known she'd purloined one of him, could he?

She pressed her shoulders back and raised her chin while trying to think of a defense. No one had told her not to take photographs of the guests dining. They'd even asked her to capture some of the dancing. Before she formed one word of her rebuttal, Titus stood two feet from her with a blank expression on his face and no message in his eyes.

So she waited.

And he stood like a statue in front of her, navy blue pin-striped cutaway suit tailored to an impeccable fit, with not even a glimmer of emotion on his face now.

"Sir, I—"

"Good eve—"

Then they laughed in unison while Amelia's shoulders relaxed, and the crinkles returned to the corners of his eyes.

"Excuse my interruption, Miss Harris. Do continue."

"No, no, absolutely no need to apologize. Please do call me Amelia."

Oh, how the lamps make his eyes twinkle.

"Out of respect, my position requires me to address all females with their titles, I'm afraid."

"Even in private? For I shouldn't mind you using my given name when we're alone."

As the last word left her tongue, heat blazed across her cheeks and over her chest. Had she really just been so brazen as to suggest they would be alone? He must this very moment assume her to be like one of the many she'd seen swooning over him in the few hours she'd been here. With a groan, she raised her left hand to the hollow spot between her collarbones and clasped her locket. "I am...I did not... Oh, goodness, what you must think of me."

Titus grasped her elbow and gave it a gentle squeeze. "Think nothing of it. I understood what you meant, Miss...Amelia. I did. I know your intentions were pure." He glanced over his shoulder and ran his gaze throughout the room before returning it to her face. With a smile that touched his eyes, he lowered his hand, then shoved it into his suit coat pocket. "Perhaps when we find ourselves in moments like this, our given names will be just fine."

She giggled. "Agreed. Now, may I ask what brought you over here?"

Several notes from the orchestra's instruments,

followed by clapping and squeals of excitement from the guests, announced the dancing would commence. Amelia should make her way to the edge of the dance-floor and prepare her camera, but not until Titus stated his business. If he hadn't been angered by her actions, then why had he joined her?

"I was trying to escape the guests who... Well, I was going outside to the courtyard to take a respite, but I noticed you standing here in the shadows alone and thought I'd check on your well-being."

"Thank you, Titus. That's very kind of you. I'm well. I'd finished my meal and couldn't resist capturing a few photographs of everyone in their elaborate attire. I know I'll be here all summer and will have plenty of opportunity for taking photographs, but there is nothing quite like the first night. I find the emotion sinks into each picture, especially when the guests are unaware I'm photographing them."

He smiled again. "I've never thought of it like that. There is something about a first, isn't there? How wonderful you have the ability to capture that memory for viewing later and for years to come. We are honored to have you here at the Grand, Amelia."

"The honor is all mine, sir."

And with that, Titus exited through the kitchen while Amelia returned to her seat with the hope the trembling in her legs would ease long enough for her to capture the essence of the evening. She'd return her camera to her room for safekeeping if someone asked her to dance.

Her tablemates no longer sat in their chairs, so they'd either gone to the dancefloor or elsewhere. Tightening her grip on her camera, she slipped the steel chain of her leather flower-embossed purse onto her wrist. She'd recovered enough from her exhilarating time with Titus to take photographs.

Then again, maybe she should retire for the evening. She had plenty of time to work this summer. Besides, with *The Hound of the Baskervilles* sitting on her nightstand, reading until she fell asleep sounded like the perfect end to her exhausting travels.

"You're wrong, Hooper. Governor Jelks will do great things for the state of Alabama." A man's sharp voice, maybe only a few feet behind her, floated over her and locked her into her chair.

"I disagree, Sherwood," another man, probably Mr. Hooper, argued.

Amelia captured her bottom lip with her teeth and sucked in her breath. If she sat still and undetected, she might be fortunate enough to learn something about the leader of her temporary home from these men who stood between her and the path to the door.

"How could you disagree? He's following Mississippi in keeping things as they should be."

"As they should be, Sherwood? Making sure the poor can't vote? Guaranteeing if a person's skin is, well, darker than ours, they can't vote? How is that right? All people who call Alabama home should be able to have a say in the state's affairs."

Amelia released her breath at a snail's pace as she set her bottom lip free. These men were arguing over the requirements a person must meet in order to be considered a valuable member of society...in the interest of suffrage? Hadn't that matter been settled in the Civil war? How would they feel about women voting?

"Hooper, if you give them a say, they'll run us. They'll stop working in the fields. They'll stop serving as our cooks and governesses and housekeepers. Jelks is doing great things. He's making certain children aren't overworked, that they are educated. Using the convicts to do railroad work. And ensuring people who get out of their place get what they deserve."

"You mean, he's doing good for the white man. And for the white children. What about the others, Sherwood?"

Why wouldn't these men move on so she could exit? They could stay in here for the rest of the night going on about their political arguments. And she wouldn't be able to resist joining in.

"Martin Hooper, you'd better not allow such talk to be heard by anyone else other than me around here. That kind of speech could get you bound, weighted, and thrown into the bay at the end of the boardwalk."

Amelia couldn't take any more of this bully's harassment. She didn't care if they knew she'd overheard them. She wouldn't sit here another minute.

She shoved her chair backward with less grace than she'd been taught to use, not caring if it rammed into the men, then stood. A quick pivot toward them revealed nothing remarkable about them except their gaping mouths, which were probably a result of their knowledge that the woman who had been invisible to them moments before had overheard them. She raked her gaze across both their faces, then bit back the words she wanted to say. Not a good idea to add a death threat to the end of this long day. She scurried from the building, watching over her shoulder until she made it safely behind her room's door.

CHAPTER 3

*I*f one more complaint reached Titus's ears, he might hop on the next delivery wagon and leave his responsibilities behind him. He had met few guests who expressed complete satisfaction. While the Grand Hotel had much to boast about, it never promised to be the Battle House in Mobile. The Grand was positioned directly on the bay, so mosquitoes, gnats, bird droppings, and the occasional snake came with the stay.

He felt the urge to return the complaints to the guests. For he could think of plenty to complain about. For starters, noisy children. Then, drunken laughter into the wee hours of the morning. He'd be remiss if he forgot his largest complaint—people tromping through the sand dunes. The *Sternula antillarum* and the *Charadrius wilsonia* nested there, among other birds.

People who didn't respect nature shouldn't spend their summers in it.

Titus's breath caught at the hitch in his heart. Why did he act as though he owned the resort? Was he the god of this breathtaking nature that surrounded him?

No, he was not.

But still... Hadn't the God of the heavens put man in charge of caring for creation? He wasn't trying to be pious. He only cared about being a good steward.

People are creations too. They must be cared for and taught how to treat nature and its animals well.

Still, nature required no forbearance, not like people did.

While his staff set up the tables on the lawn for the Sunday afternoon meal beneath the bent oaks, Titus resumed his rounds, leaving behind the boardwalk, the gulls, and the glassy bay. By year's end, if all went according to his plan, he'd be at Frank Chapman's Christmas Bird Count participating in the census of winter bird populations and not having to be bothered by any of this.

After the lunch hour passed, the guests rested beneath the oaks in the shade, splashed in the bay, or played tennis or charades. Titus could escape to the dunes at the far end of the property. Once he had changed into his gray trousers and blue-striped vest—leaving his coat behind for the afternoon—he donned his pull-on boots. Seizing his binoculars and fedora, he dashed out the back entrance of his cottage for his adventure.

If he made enough notations about the plovers and the terns in his notebook and kept studying the behaviors of these seabirds, he could potentially meet the qualifications for a position as a warden at one of the newly established wildlife refuges along the Florida coast. No more wearing suits every day. No more...

As Titus stepped onto the sandy path leading to the dunes, he groaned. There he went again placing a higher regard for birds over people. That mindset wouldn't allow him to succeed at anything. For if he couldn't associate freely with humans, the very ones who could put him in the positions he desired, then he would never be a warden or an important part of Audubon.

You need people. They need you. No amount of running will change that.

Titus found a seat on a tree trunk that had fallen during a spring storm, then stretched his legs out. With the temperature already in the high nineties, he wouldn't last out here long without needing refreshment. But the quiet... That was all the refreshment he needed right now.

"Oh, goodness. Oh my! Oh!"

At the intrusion into Titus's solitude by a woman stomping through the dunes to the north, his brow furrowed and his mood soured.

Why? Why did people continue to barge their way into his world? Why was no place sacred anymore?

Titus shoved off the tree trunk while clamping his jaw shut to prevent any unkind words from slipping through his lips. What did he say to this woman who held no regard for nature that wouldn't damage his reputation and result in his dismissal?

Did he care? Maybe saying something that would send him on his way earlier than he'd anticipated was exactly what he should do.

"Oh, Lord, your creation is so beautiful!"

Titus halted and raised the binoculars that hung around his neck to his eyes. He turned the focusing wheel with his thumb until the lenses focused on the woman north of him.

That face.

That smile.

The glee that showed in her eyes—eyes that matched her sky-blue skirt.

Amelia Harris.

She stood with camera strap around her neck, surveying the view, both hands grasping her cheeks. Had she never before seen dunes? Maybe she'd never seen the sea oats blowing in the breeze? Or perhaps it was the plovers and terns on their nests that struck her with awe?

When her gaze met his and she raised one hand in a wave, Titus dropped the binoculars as he gulped. She'd caught him admiring her. What would she think of his boldness?

"Mr. Overton! Good afternoon," she yelled across the dunes as she stomped her way through them toward him.

Shoving down the heat which rose in his chest both from the sight of her beauty but also from the fury over her disregard for this refuge, he raised his hand toward her. Not in a wave but to halt her. "Miss Harris, please, don't take another step!"

"What?" She froze.

"Your footsteps. They damage the landscape of the dunes. If you don't watch where your shoes land, you could crush eggs in nests. Eggs of the migratory birds."

"Oh." She lowered her gaze to the sand beneath her feet.

Titus did the same. As he drew nearer, minding each footstep, he verified she had somehow avoided damaging any of the nests. He smiled as the tension in his shoulders eased. Then he met her gaze expecting a returned smile.

But instead, she squinted at him, both hands now on her hips. No smile touched her rose-colored lips.

He'd offended her, hadn't he?

Of course he had. Only a fool wouldn't see it.

"Mr. Overton, how should someone know if they should or shouldn't venture into the dunes or how to proceed if they do if there are no signs giving instructions? No barrier of sorts to keep people out of them?

Have I broken some kind of wildlife protection law I wasn't aware of? I hardly think you can hold me accountable for something I knew nothing about."

"Miss—"

"It seems awfully presumptuous of you to assume your guests would—"

"Miss—"

"—know the rules about all the places here on the property without some sort of announcement or circular stating the rules of behavior. It truly—"

"Miss Harris! May I speak?" Sweat dripped down both sides of his face as the afternoon sun scorched the back of his neck. Or was the burn from the ceaseless scolding from this woman?

She dropped her hands by her sides, then nodded.

"You are correct that there should be signs or a circular or at least an announcement to the guests about venturing off into the dunes without a guide. I'll see to it that it's done. These guidelines are as much for the safety of the wildlife as they are for our guests. It certainly isn't because we don't want you to enjoy the beauty that can be seen only from inside them."

She regarded the dunes almost as if taking them in for the first time again, then returned her gaze to his. "I simply wanted to see if I should start my photography work here in the dunes tomorrow morning. I felt certain the sunrise would bring excellent light and shading across the landscape. And I'm positive I might capture the flowers awakening as well as the birds."

Titus smiled again. So she didn't have a disregard for the things that touched his heart. Quite the opposite. But her unawareness...

"You're quite right again. But you must also be aware we have rattlers and copperheads, quite poisonous snakes, which sometimes come into the dunes looking for a meal of eggs and hatchlings. We've also had the occasional alligator."

Amelia closed the distance between them and grasped his right forearm. "Did you...did you say...alli...alligators?"

A chuckle burst from Titus as he patted her warm hand. "I did, indeed. And that's why you must not come into the dunes unescorted."

She cut her gaze toward him out of the corner of her eye. "Mr. Overton, if I didn't know any better, I'd think you were trying to frighten me."

"Not at all, Miss Harris. I want to keep all my guests safe, for when they return home to their family and friends, I want them to speak only of the beauty and rest they found here. That's how we ensure they return and their acquaintances join them."

She slipped her hand from his arm, leaving a cold spot in its place, then faced him. "Mr.—Titus— perhaps you should appoint someone to accompany me on my walks so I can capture the beautiful nature around me without endangering it or myself."

A gust of wind blew across them, lifting both their

hats from their heads. Titus grasped his hat, then snatched hers before it landed in the sand.

As he handed it to her, their gazes meeting once again, the world fell silent around him. His heartbeat drowned out the screeches of the gulls and pelicans. Could she hear it too?

Despite his parched mouth and throat, he croaked against the wind, "Miss—well, Amelia—perhaps I myself will escort you on your walks, for I don't know of another gentleman here in Point Clear with more knowledge of its feathered inhabitants as well as the four-legged ones." Titus's cheeks burned, and his legs felt as though they'd betray him and dump him onto the sand right in front of Amelia.

Had he really volunteered his time and presence to her?

Clearly, more than his legs were threatening to betray him today.

～

"Oh, Titus, I know your time is much too important to chaperone me while I work. I plan to photograph at all hours and in every place I can safely get to. I wouldn't dream of asking you to—"

"Amelia, you didn't ask. I offered."

Raising her right eyebrow and cocking her head sideways, she leaned toward him. "Are you sure you're not simply trying to keep me out of trouble? And by way of that, keep yourself out of trouble with the owner of the resort?"

Another chuckle launched from his throat and sent tingles to her toes. "Maybe. Maybe a tad bit."

"As I suspected." She nodded. "How about we strike a bargain? When I'm ready to venture into the dunes again, I'll inform you the night before so you can appoint someone to accompany me or join me yourself?"

Despite her original plans to create no entanglements while here this summer, time spent with Titus while venturing among the beauty surrounding them wouldn't be the worst experience.

She stifled a giggle.

"Agreed. Now allow me to escort you out of the dunes." He extended his arm to her.

As she placed her hand in the warm crook of his elbow, she focused her gaze on the sand. Careful footsteps would protect more than the creatures. "While we walk, perhaps you could share with me what brought you to have such a heart for nature."

Titus's arm tightened underneath her hand, and silence fell upon them. Had she offended him with her question? Pried into his private affairs? They had only known each other less than a full day. She had no right to know his motives for anything he did. No right to intrude into his life.

Before she could retract her question and let him out of the obligation he most assuredly felt to answer her, he responded in a low voice almost drowned out by the wind.

"The reasons for my respect of and love for nature are too numerous to explain during one walk. I suppose, to put it in a nice parcel for you, I spent my childhood on a farm in Mississippi with cows, horses, pigs, chickens, ducks, goats, and of course, dogs and cats. They were all my pets, as far as I saw it. I had my best conversations with some of them."

"You, a farmer's son? I would have never guessed it. You are so...refined."

Titus nodded, not seeming to take offense to her complement. For it had been a compliment and not a slander against farmers.

"My father taught me much about caring for the animals, and about slaughtering them as well, when the time came."

Amelia tightened her grip on his arm as the harsh words touched her ears.

"I know it has to be done. We must eat. We benefit from the byproducts of the farm animals, but I never grew accustomed to being part of it. My father considered me weak. When my mother defended me, well, it wasn't a favorable situation."

"I'm so sorry, Titus." That's all she offered. She didn't want this man, still so much a stranger to her, to feel the need to guard himself around her or to be disingenuous.

"My father's brother, my uncle Sidney, had sold his

farm adjacent to ours some five or so years earlier and moved his family to the city, to Mobile. He wanted to be a part of the progress that was taking place. When I reached the age of fifteen, I asked if I could go live with my uncle. My mother had passed the year before from cholera, and Papa had taken to drowning his sorrows in a bottle. I couldn't stay."

"What happened when you asked to leave?"

Titus paused at the end of the path, the guest-covered lawn no more than fifty feet away from them. He pivoted and faced her.

She dropped her hand from his arm and clasped her camera. Would he tell her the rest? Or leave her suspended in curiosity until they were alone again—if that moment ever came again?

"Papa told me to go. He drove me to the train station in Columbus and said his goodbyes. I suppose I'd disappointed him most of my life, and he'd been expecting me to leave eventually."

"So your love for preserving animals drove you away from the farm, but you ended up in the city where animals in nature were scarce?"

"Indeed. But there, at least, I didn't have to participate in the demise of the animals. And I still found spots that hadn't been destroyed by buildings where I could enjoy my surroundings. My uncle sent me to school, and that's how I learned so much about protecting endangered animals, trees, and other plant life."

"I see. Seems the change resulted in good things for you and for your surroundings."

"I suppose it did."

"And it would appear the dear Lord placed the perfect person here to protect His creation from unaware people such as myself." She smiled up at Titus, although he'd already shifted back into his role as manager of the resort and didn't see her expression.

"Forgive my rudeness, Miss Harris. I must attend to the commotion that appears to be happening between two of our most prominent guests."

And with that, Titus was gone.

CHAPTER 4

*F*rom Amelia's spot on a bench beneath the oaks, she scanned her surroundings. Families bustled about the lawn, children protesting having to leave playtime for dinner preparations. The birds which nibbled an evening meal from the ground escaped the stampede for the high branches above her. Not having children to tend to afforded Amelia a moment of rest before dinner, and she counted every passing minute with a smile.

By the end of her third day at the Grand, she'd photographed the Maguires, the McAvoys, the Sullivans, and the Whitmores. She'd captured the portraits of the owner, Reuben Kroyer, and his family, the waitstaff, and the chef and his staff. The new camera *The Photographic Times* had sent with her required less time between photographs than the model she had used on her last assignment, which meant her subjects could smile and children didn't have to sit still for as long or be bound while waiting for the picture to take.

By week's end, she could set up her darkroom. She'd inquire of Titus where he felt it should be. Along with the portraits she'd taken for some of the large families staying in the hotel and the ones taken for the management, she'd develop the roll she'd taken in the dining hall—the roll that contained the photograph of Titus. If it had blurred or wasn't suitable enough to hold her memory of him, she'd most assuredly have to take another one.

Why? You don't need a memory of a man you'll never see again once you leave. No attachments, remember?

Regardless, Titus would be the one to advise her where to set everything up since she'd already made his acquaintance and since he managed the resort. Although, his offer of assistance could have meant he would assign one of his employees to aid her. She'd understand if that were the case.

But he had offered to help, so maybe he'd meant he would personally assist her.

Amelia Harris! Stop woolgathering about this man.

Amelia puffed a stray strand of hair out of her face, then sighed.

Whether she became a friend or remained only an acquaintance, she longed to hear more of his story. More about how he'd gone from farm to city and then to seashore. Even more, she hoped to hear further details of how he overcame his father's criticism—rejection, really—and went on to become the manager of the resort.

His behavior when he'd found her in the dunes proved he still cared about animals, maybe even more than he cared about people. The man was filled with mystery. And if she was afforded another chance to see him in private, maybe she'd solve some of that mystery.

The smile that tugged at her mouth disappeared as her mind sent out another warning to her heart.

If she'd been the cynical kind, she would have thought Titus had been avoiding her since their walk in the dunes. He had yet to make an appointment for his portrait, and when she'd seen him in the dining hall the last two nights, he hadn't ventured her way or even glanced in her direction.

But she wouldn't let runaway thoughts root ideas in her mind that simply might not be true. Titus Overton was far too busy a man to spend much time thinking about her. And she should make certain she remained equally as occupied so her thoughts of him would cease.

Smoothing her hands down the front of her mauve tea dress, she left the shady spot beneath the oaks and made her way to the path. Her corset and other undergarments caused perspiration to begin as soon as the sun hit her body. Thankfully, the maid, Bessie, had agreed not to cinch the laces to their limits. Amelia didn't care if her figure wasn't as *S*-shaped as the other women's. Being able to breathe and not suffocate in this heat mattered more to her than fashion.

With fifteen minutes to spare before dinner, she should arrive at the dining hall with enough time to find a table that hadn't filled to capacity yet. Before coming, she hadn't given enough thought to the fact she might be the only one at the resort without friends or family to dine with. That did appear to be the case. Dining alone didn't bother her, for she enjoyed watching families interact with each other and didn't mind not having to carry the conversation. However, an entire summer of dining alone might have ill effects on her. Not to mention, an unattached woman her age alone every evening could wind up being prey for unscrupulous men.

Perhaps she should make a friend or two.

Amelia sped her pace toward the dining hall as her stomach growled. What would they serve tonight? Last night's crawfish and alligator tail had been her first experience with an atypical meat source, and with cayenne pepper, and none of it had settled too well on her stomach. She'd had to take a dose of magnesia before feeling better. Hopefully, tonight's meal would be a bit tamer.

"Miss photographer, may I have a moment?"

At the mention of her job title, Amelia halted and pivoted toward the gentleman with her hands clasped in front of her. "Yes?"

He nodded. "Sorry, I didn't know your name."

Guests stepped off the path, passing them, then returned to it.

Amelia hadn't thought until this moment how they must all look like cattle coming into the barn at day's end. She stifled a giggle. "Amelia Harris." She offered her hand, and the man accepted it with a gentle shake.

But when he held tight, she slid her gaze to his eyes as his familiarity dawned on her. Although she'd seen him in the dimness of the dining hall and not in full daylight when she'd first encountered him, it only took a second glance to recognize him.

Mr. Sherwood. The man who had threatened Mr. Hooper at dinner.

Stifling the desire to scream, Amelia tugged her hand free from Mr. Sherwood's, then squinted at him. "How can I be of assistance to you?"

"You recognize me, correct?"

"I'm sure our paths may have crossed somewhere at the resort."

The corner of his mouth lifted in a smirk, one that looked more like an evil sneer.

Amelia resisted the urge to run away even though shivers of warning danced up and down her spine.

"Miss Harris, I believe you overheard a conversation I had with one of my acquaintances, Mr. Hooper, which might have sounded more ominous than it was intended."

Amelia took a step back, creating some space

between herself and Mr. Sherwood, but he advanced and stood even closer to her.

"Sir, I've heard many conversations over the last few days, and in the weeks prior during my travels. I make it my business not to mind other people's business. So I assure you, if I overheard anything, it is of no matter to me. Now if you'll allow me, I'd like to get to the dining hall before the meal is cold." Pivoting away from this rude man, she sucked in her breath and pressed her shoulders back.

But when he grabbed her forearm and brought her to a full stop, the fear that mixed with anger in her gut resulted in an exhale strong enough to knock the man's hat off—had he been wearing one on his oversized head.

"Excuse me? Release me at once!"

"Miss..." He yanked her closer. "I'm quite sure you remember me and you remember the conversation. For the distress in your lovely blue eyes and the stain on your supple cheeks contradict your words."

Amelia yanked her arm away from him and stepped back. Should she scream? Should she threaten to call Titus, the only man she knew more than anyone else here?

No! She didn't need a man to rescue her.

"Miss Harris, it would be in your best interest to forget anything you may have heard. Or should I say *overheard*. Forget having met me."

She released a bellow as she tossed her head backward, then directed her gaze at him, shooting daggers his way with the hopes he would never approach her again. "Sir, I believe you think more highly of yourself than you should, for I already stated I didn't remember you or any conversation you had in my presence." While she spoke a lie, this was one that surely even the good Lord would forgive. "Now, however, you've created a permanent memory in my mind I won't quickly forget. I believe, perhaps, it might be in *your* best interest to forget having met me. After all, I do work for a popular news source. One that might love a story about a man who threatened an innocent woman. I may not know who you are, but I'd wager there are plenty of people here who do. So why don't we agree to steer clear of each other? That would work out in favor of both of us."

She pivoted and marched toward the dining hall without giving Mr. Sherwood a chance to interject, never looking back to see if he followed her.

∿

Titus held the door open for the swarm of guests coming into the dining hall, nodding his greetings and adding as many salutations as he could before they passed him. As much as he longed for the quiet of some coastal island where he could count the bird population or monitor loggerhead turtles, he couldn't deny the tingles that filled him when guests arrived for the evening festivities dressed in more than their Sunday best. Was it the food that brought them in with smiles on their faces? The prospects of meeting people? The promise of an encounter with someone that could change their futures?

Titus shrugged as the last guest entered the hall. It didn't matter what brought the smiles, as long as those smiles came. When guests were happy, the owners were happy. And that meant less strife for him.

If only he could experience a portion of their pleasure. He felt like a palm frond stuck in the ground after a summer storm. Completely stuck here. With no way to find what he was looking for. Sure, a woman might bring a certain level of contentment to his heart...for a while...but if she left—as Evelyn had—the devastation would take joy's place. He was better off engaging his mind and not his heart this summer, then getting out of here.

"Miss Harris! Do not walk away from me while I am speaking to you. Do you realize who I am?"

The sharp words sliced through the evening air and plunged into Titus. Who was speaking to a woman with such a tone?

Miss Harris?

Not just any woman.

Amelia Harris!

Titus left behind the delight the guests had showered him with only moments before and rushed toward Amelia and whoever chased after her. But as he stomped down the path and drew closer to the pair, uncertainty pulled him in several directions. Switching his gaze from Amelia to the man who followed her, the awareness that she might not want his help filled him. After all, she'd come here alone. Wasn't she capable of defending herself?

With graceful shoulders pushed back and chin held high, the woman stared in his direction. She wasn't yet close enough for him to discern the expression on her face, couldn't tell if her legs quivered beneath her silken dress. From this distance, she seemed fully capable of managing the situation without his aid.

"I said, don't walk away from me!" The red-faced man had caught up to her. With a swift sweep of his hand, he grabbed Amelia by the arm and jerked her around to face him, knocking her off the path and onto the grass.

And that settled it for him. No man treated any woman that way, especially not on Titus's watch.

He increased his pace and was now less than sixty feet from them. Heat burned in his chest and poured out his ears, which now rang so loudly he couldn't hear a word they said to each other.

Perhaps this man was an acquaintance of Amelia's and not someone she'd just met? Maybe this was a lover's quarrel, and he should stay out of it?

Titus shook his head as he closed the distance between them. No matter who that man was to her, he had no right to treat her that way. He had stood idly by while Papa mistreated Mother. He would not let this man treat Amelia like this and do nothing about it.

"Pardon me, but—"

"This doesn't concern you." The man held his hand out to Titus.

Did the ingrate think that would stop Titus from coming to the assistance of one of his female guests?

"Excuse me, but any quarrel between any of my guests—"

"*Your* guests?" The man pivoted toward Titus as he kept his grasp tight on Amelia's arm.

When their gazes locked, Titus froze mid-step.

Mr. Lloyd Sherwood, Sherwood of Rhode Island, was Amelia's rival?

Of course, he would come to her aid against one of the most influential men in the South. But he couldn't back down now. Couldn't let Sherwood see him weaken. Couldn't let Amelia remain in danger.

"Yes, *my* guests. I'm not sure if you're aware, but I'm general manager here, and it's my duty to ensure all guests are safe and satisfied. I don't know what you were quarreling about, but I assure you, it must cease now. We'll not have such behavior upsetting the atmosphere of this place."

Sherwood snorted. "Do you know who I am?"

Amelia jerked her arm from Sherwood's grasp and crossed her arms in front of her.

Titus slid his gaze to hers.

With her lips tied into a tight pink bow and cheeks

stained red, she glared at him. Was her fury directed at
him for defending her? Or was she still fuming from
Sherwood's assault?

Titus returned his gaze to Sherwood. If Amelia was
angry with him, if he'd somehow played an unwanted
hero, then he wouldn't do it again. But he couldn't
retreat now without losing his authority over this
abusive man.

"I know who you are, and it is of no consequence to
me. You may command admiration and preferential
treatment where you come from, but here at the Grand,
we treat all guests with the same respect. Male or
female. Mogul or servant. Makes no difference." Titus
spread his feet farther apart, then locked his knees.

Would Sherwood attempt to display his domi-
nance? Lay a finger on him? If so, would Titus defend
himself or back down?

Titus squinted at Sherwood while cocking his chin
upward. Oh, he would defend himself. He could not let
someone like this win. Not in the presence of such a
fine woman as Amelia.

"You may hold a place of importance here at the
resort, Mr. Overton, but where I come from, you're
nothing, a nobody, of no importance. No one in the
world outside of Point Clear has even heard your
name." Sherwood's words came out in mists of anger
that sprayed onto Titus's face. "So I recommend you
stay here for the rest of your days because if you ever
attempt to venture to another resort or to somewhere

like New York or Boston or Philadelphia where I am not only known but revered, you'll find yourself washing dishes or emptying the garbage instead of managing anything or anyone."

"Threats. This man only knows how to spew threats." Amelia glared at Sherwood, her hands folded across her stomach. "I am from Philadelphia, and I've never heard your name before I came here."

Titus slid his handkerchief from his pocket and wiped the remnants of Sherwood's words from his face. Although he could drag him behind the woodshed right now and teach him a lesson he'd never forget, Titus curbed his anger and chose to heed the knot in his belly. He'd serve himself and his guests better if he let Sherwood win this round. Or at least think he won.

Titus stepped off the path onto the grass and motioned for Sherwood to depart from them.

"That's what I thought you'd do. Good decision, Mr. Overton." Sherwood gave a quick glance in Amelia's direction before following the path to the dining hall.

He wasted no time attending to Amelia. "Are you—"

"Of course I am!" Her hands now rested on her hips, and her gaze sparkled with fire.

"Well, I—"

"Mr. Overton, I'm not a child. I can handle a disagreement without assistance."

Titus stepped closer to her, leaning forward so his voice didn't require much volume. While no other guests remained on the lawn, he didn't want to exhibit an act two for anyone who might be within hearing range. "Amelia, that powerful man had his hand on you, an unchaperoned woman at least twenty years his junior. If he'd do something like that out in the open for all to see, then what could he..." Titus choked down the bile which burned his throat. "...would he do if he found you in private? I could not stand by and watch him berate you any further. If I have offended you, then I offer my apologies. But I do not regret my actions. Nor do I understand your opposition to them."

She studied his face, the fire in her eyes dwindling into a mere smolder. As her arms dropped to her sides, her shoulders eased and the tension in her face seemed to roll off. "Thank...thank you...for coming to my defense, Titus." Her lips quivered as a tear streamed from her right eye.

He stepped closer. He hadn't intended—

She raised her hand to halt him. "I appreciate you making sure I'm not harmed in any way—especially in the worst way—but if I let men like that glimpse any weakness in me and think I need to be rescued, they'll either continue to perceive me as nothing more than an inferior being because I'm a woman and will, therefore, continue to treat me as such, or they'll consider it a personal challenge to become my savior."

She swiped another tear from her face. "As you know, I didn't have the smoothest of transitions when I arrived. Well, that's behind me. I'm strong and won't let men like Mr. Sherwood strip me of my confidence."

Amelia gave Titus a quick nod, then stepped onto the path and headed toward the dining hall. Sand billowed as her skirts brushed across the ground.

A strong woman, she was.

And she'd made her point clear. While here in Point Clear, she didn't need his assistance.

CHAPTER 5

*A*melia might not have yet made acquaintances with many of the women her age, for most of them were already married and tending to their children, or filling their time with tennis and pinocle while their governesses minded the offspring, but she had steadily collected a following of both boys and girls between the ages of thirteen and seventeen over the last few days. Armed with their own cameras or sketch paper, they waited outside her door underneath the oaks for her each morning and accompanied her on her walks around the property.

She'd first set her camera on its stand and taken as many shots of Mobile Bay at sunrise and the hour or so afterward before the breakfast bell rang through the resort the day after her arrival. On the third morning of doing such, she'd discovered two wide-eyed children watching her. Two days later, Mae O'Hare and Stanley

Palmer joined her. Their own cameras dangled around their necks, making words unnecessary.

They'd kept coming every day for the last week, and they'd brought their cousins and friends with them. This morning was no different, as they stood at the shoreline capturing pictures of everything in sight.

It hadn't taken long for Amelia to focus her camera on smaller and smaller objects, and now, she not only photographed flowers but also the individual petals, stems, and other parts of their anatomy. The sea oats, the crabs, the tiny shells that washed up every morning... She couldn't capture enough of them.

"Miss Amelia?"

"Yes, Mae?"

With hair like cinnamon and eyes like emeralds, Mae grinned. "When are you going to take us on an adventure? We've come to the shoreline every morning for a week. Before that, we walked the paths and watched birds and squirrels. Learned about the plant life. We're ready for more."

Amelia stepped away from her camera, a smile tugging at both her heart and her lips. "An adventure, you say? An adventure sounds quite lovely, doesn't it? I hear the director of entertainment planned an outing to Fort Morgan for tomorrow. I thought I might go. Wouldn't that make a fine Saturday outing?"

Stanley hopped on his toes, freckles strewn across his cheeks and ebony curls tumbling onto his forehead. "A fort? A real one?" His voice cracked.

Amelia smiled at the boy whose torso hadn't caught up with his arms and legs yet. "That's right. I've seen photographs of it and would love to take some of my own. Perhaps you could ask your father or mother to accompany you."

Stanley shook his head. "Father won't come with me. He has no interest in such outings. Besides, it would be more fun if you chaperoned me."

"I want to go," Goldie Quinn chimed in, her smile casting more light onto Amelia than the morning's glow.

"Me too!" Willis Sharp jumped forward, almost knocking Goldie off balance.

Amelia hated to douse their fire of exuberance, but *The Photographic Times* hadn't sent her here as a nanny. And while many of the guests might find pleasure in sending their children off for a day-long excursion, she didn't want the responsibility of making sure no one fell overboard or lost a battle with a jellyfish—especially not of four children.

"I would gladly accept your company on the adventure, but I must insist your parents or someone they approve of chaperone you. I am on assignment while here and cannot take on such a responsibility."

"Miss Amelia, we won't cause trouble. We'll bring our cameras and our best behaviors." Mae grabbed her left arm and tugged.

"We promise." Goldie grabbed her other arm and pleaded with eyes the color of a cloudy morning sky, her walnut-colored braided ponytail swinging over her shoulder and landing across her left collarbone.

Before Amelia had the chance to form her rebuttal on her tongue, the breakfast bell rang and saved her. "Looks like we'll have to continue this conversation at another time. Run along to breakfast, lest your parents think a pirate stole away with you."

Despite their moans and groans, they abandoned her at the shore in pursuit of more immediate satisfaction.

Sucking in a salt-infused breath, she accepted her victory.

Then Amelia's stomach growled, reminding her she hadn't eaten a snack at bedtime last night. What would they serve this morning? More eggs and bacon, no doubt. But biscuits and gravy might be the first things she partook of if they offered them.

As Amelia packed her camera and stand in her case, droplets of rain pelted her back. She hadn't noticed the clouds rolling in off the bay, but a quick glance upward revealed a heavy storm would hit them soon. She wouldn't have time to take her case to her room, then make it to the dining hall before the torrent arrived, so she clamped it shut, picked up her skirt, and scampered up the slope to the grass. Although being soaked from head to toe meant looking like a half-drowned seabird, her skin tingled beneath her white blouse as the rain landed on her and made her feel like one of the children who had just left her.

Young. Carefree. Not a single worry.

Maybe after breakfast if the rain continued, she'd set up her camera beneath the pavilion on the bay and capture some of nature's finest moments.

A day of rain could also provide an opportunity to set up her darkroom, which she needed to do because some of the guests she'd photographed were leaving at the end of next week and they wanted to take their portraits with them. Since she hadn't spoken with Titus even once in the last eleven days, and he did not even come close enough to her for them to exchange so much as a nod or smile, she'd ask for someone else's help. After all, she shouldn't trouble the general manager with such menial tasks, especially after she'd told him she didn't need rescuing.

Regret tightened around her heart. She hadn't meant to offend him, but she must have.

No, you're imagining things.

Amelia brushed the regret away as she ran the last twenty feet to the dining hall, trying not to slip on the wet grass. She thought too highly of herself if she thought Titus had redirected his path to avoid someone he'd known only a few days and had spoken to as many times.

As Amelia reached the path, she focused her gaze toward the door. When it landed on Titus, standing there in his black suit holding the door open for the scurrying guests, her heart squeezed. She owed him an apology for her brashness. She'd speak with him before breakfast if he had time.

When his gaze met hers, though, his face relaxed from the smile he'd held moments before, then he slipped into the building, leaving a male guest holding the door.

Amelia halted as her chest took on the weight of a hundred beasts. Either she'd wounded Titus more than she'd imagined, or she'd misjudged him and he was, in fact, a heartless and chauvinistic man. Either way, she wanted nothing to do with him. Nor did she even want breakfast anymore.

She pivoted and ran around the back of the building to her room. The tears that stung her eyes rivaled the rain now beating against her back like the fiercest of enemies.

Why did Titus's rejection hurt her so much? Why did she care what a near-stranger thought of her? She might have offended him, but he'd just insulted her with his actions. Any man who would do such a thing to a lady didn't deserve this kind of emotional response in her. And yet, the torrent of tears flooded her face and thunderous sobs burst from her mouth as she slammed her suite door behind her.

$\sim$

*T*itus pushed past the guests who seemed not to care how long it took them to get to their tables. They lingered among friends with smiles on their faces while he fought the perspiration that burst out all over his body at the mere sight of Amelia. He'd suffocate if he didn't get outside to the staff courtyard immediately. While he couldn't have avoided seeing her for much longer, the last eleven days had been the only reprieve from his heart's awakening that he'd had since his gaze first landed on her.

He hadn't wanted this. And yet it had come, anyway.

Someone kept trying to derail his plans, kept trying to prove him wrong in his belief that he didn't need entanglements with people. Was it the God the minister had spoken about last Sunday morning at the service at the pavilion? Titus hadn't actually attended. He'd set out chairs for extra guests and overheard the minister relate how God had rescued the people of Israel from slavery to the Egyptians. Then He'd commanded them not to worship other gods because He was jealous of anything or anyone that took His place.

Why would people believe in such a demanding being?

If this God was the one trying to make him miserable, what purpose would He have in causing Titus to long for the company of another woman? Wasn't he miserable enough after his loss? God had clearly taken Evelyn from him because of His jealousy. So why would

He taunt him with the likes of Amelia Harris? Was this a cruel joke this Creator played on His unsuspecting subjects?

It didn't make sense. Plenty of people were married and found love. Why would this God try to keep Titus from finding that same kind of happiness?

Titus burst through the back door and ran to his cottage, dodging the pelting rain. Fighting the anger which made his blood feel as though it was boiling, he bolted up his steps, then thrust himself onto the porch swing. Even the musky smell of the rain-infused air couldn't calm him right now. He didn't want to need people, and he certainly didn't want to need a God who took away those whom Titus loved.

The rain intensified, wind blowing in his direction and spraying mist across him. A cool mist. Not typical of a mid-June day. Titus closed his eyes and inhaled the fragrance of freshness. After ten or so seconds, he exhaled through his mouth, keeping his eyes closed. He didn't want to look at the world right now. He just wanted to feel the breeze, to pretend no one else but him existed.

Why were his arms and legs so heavy?

Why did he need to force every breath?

Why wasn't he refreshed?

A crack of lightning, then a crash of something onto the ground thrust Titus's eyes open and his body to his feet. The porch swing hit the railing as its chain creaked in resistance. The lightning had struck a live oak fifteen feet from his porch and brought one of its branches to the ground.

Clasping the railing, Titus couldn't blink, couldn't swallow. He kept his gaze locked on the branch, the branch he'd marched under minutes before.

What if...

What if he'd been...

With a shake of his head, he released his grip on the railing, then ran his hands through his hair. That could have been him. The lightning could have struck him and brought his death.

His arms and legs no longer felt heavy. Instead, they tingled with a similar jolt to what had hit the tree limb. He was alive and fortunate to be that way.

Why had he let his responsibilities here and his grief over losing Evelyn steal his love for living?

Each day seemed like a repeat of the day before—waking with a desire to start living one day when...when he wasn't here anymore. But waiting to live wasn't living at all. It was no different than waiting to die.

And that had to change. He needed a break from the resort. Just one day away to do something that could restore his zeal. But where could he go? What could he do?

Titus went inside his cottage to change out of his wet suit, visions of time away dancing across his mind and heart.

CHAPTER 6

$\mathcal{T}$itus smiled at his reflection in the mirror. How long had it been since he'd left the cottage in anything other than his morning suit or tuxedo? Today's ride on the bay boat to Fort Morgan—and time away from the resort—called for his gray sailing pants and seersucker day coat. With a nod and a quick adjustment of his waxed mustache, Titus grabbed his white straw bowler hat off the table beside the door and snapped it onto his head. Plucking his binoculars from the same table, he hung them around his neck by their cord.

On the porch, he gave another nod, this time to Sebastian and Bart as they sawed at the mammoth tree limb on his lawn. He almost hated to see it go, for it would forever serve as a reminder that life was too short not to seize every opportunity. But Mr. Kroyer wouldn't allow such a thing to stay, even if it was in the staff area. He was a stickler for keeping everything manicured.

Despite the thickness of the morning air, the sky held few clouds and promised to remain clear while he and some of the other guests took the hour-long trip across the bay to the end of the peninsula. He tingled from his head to his toes with anticipation over spotting more birds than he normally saw at the Point plus the prospect of seeing and feeding a dolphin or two. Not to mention, a stroll around the brick fort always refreshed him.

Today, with the wind blowing across his body and the sun kissing his face, he was guaranteed replenishment. Nothing could quench his joy. Nothing.

Titus strode around the side of the main building, where he joined the others. The director of entertainment, Mack Duncan, would act as guide and manager on the tour, so Titus didn't have to do anything except lean on the railing and soak in the glistening view.

"Mr. Overton, might I have a word with you?"

Titus froze mid-step with one foot dangling in the air at the sound of Reuben Kroyer's voice. Only one man's voice did he dread more than Uncle Sidney's, and that man stood behind him right now.

"Yes, sir?" Titus pivoted, facing Mr. Kroyer, who was dressed in his finest attire. The man hadn't figured out after all these years at the resort that one didn't have to wear one's evening tuxedo to breakfast, even if he did own the place.

"Mr. Overton, since you're going to Fort Morgan today, we'd like you to supervise some of the guests." This wasn't a request despite the pleasant smile pasted across Kroyer's hairless face.

"Supervise? Sir, I'm not on duty today."

Kroyer clapped him on the back, then drew him closer with an arm draped across his back and a hand clasped tightly to his right shoulder. "Titus, while we're in the height of guest season, we never really have a day to ourselves, now, do we?" He eased his grip enough to cock his chin toward him.

Titus could feel his dark gaze staring at him out of the corner of his eyes.

"This will bode well for both of us. When the guests are happy, we are happy." Kroyer clapped him on the back again, then faced him. "Be a good chap and supervise these youngsters who want to accompany the photographer lady on the tour."

Titus's eyes could pop out of his head. He tried to swallow down his... What was it he felt? Shock? Dread? No, it was something else he couldn't define.

"Miss Harris is going on the tour?"

"She is. She and her young protégées. And you will make sure they return safely."

"Sir, I...it has occurred to me just now I need to spend the day inventorying our supplies. We may be running low on items for the toilette and...and eggs." He tapped his chin and directed his gaze at Kroyer, trying to bring warmth to the look that felt cold and fierce right now.

"Mr. Overton, those things can wait until you return this afternoon." With those final words, Kroyer left him standing there with the other guests, four of whom were adolescents. These must be the charges for the day.

But where was Amelia? Perhaps she'd encountered an issue with her equipment and decided to stay—

"Good morning, Mr. Overton. I hadn't imagined you'd be joining us today."

At the curtness in Amelia's voice behind him, a mixture of hot and cold blood ran through him, warring to either freeze his veins or burst them into flames.

Titus brought his trembling right hand to his forehead and swiped away the sweat that spilled from under his hat's brim. Then, loosening his tie—why was his collar so tight?—he pasted on a smile and faced her.

He hadn't expected her arched eyebrow or her hands on her hips, but why did it surprise him? The woman was made of pure spice.

"Good morning, Miss Harris. I hadn't imagined you'd be on the tour either." What should he say next?

What would *she* say next? Would she pick up her skirt and scurry back to her room? He certainly couldn't leave as long as she was coming along because he had to chaperone her protégés.

"I...my...I'm told you have a few junior photographers that need chaperoning. I'm the designated chaperone."

A smile lit up her face as she clapped her hands. "Oh, they received permission to come along? Thank you for volunteering to—"

"I didn't volunteer." He huffed, although he hadn't meant to sound so smug. "I took one of my personal days and found out only minutes ago that chaperoning was my only option if I wanted to take the tour." Sliding his handkerchief out of his pocket, he removed his hat, then wiped his brow. Maybe a cloudless day wasn't the best kind of day for a boat ride. If he couldn't stop perspiring this early, he'd be soaked by the time they returned.

Amelia's hand on his left forearm jolted him back to his surroundings. "Titus." She leaned closer. "I owe you an apology." Her eyes glistened while her cheeks turned into perfect rose petals.

"An apology? Whatever for?"

She released his arm and lowered her gaze to the ground. After a few majestic flutters of her eyelids, she pointed her sky-like orbs at him again. "I was rude and completely ungrateful and unladylike when you came to my defense with Mr. Sherwood. I wanted to say—"

"No, don't. You have nothing to apologize for."

"But I do, Titus. I do. I am very appreciative of your assistance that day. I'm afraid my pride caused me to speak out of turn."

Titus relaxed his shoulders and smiled at her.

"Amelia, you had every right to say what you said. Times aren't as they've always been. Women are fighting for their rights to be so much more than their ancestors were ever allowed to be. I'm afraid I'm still getting accustomed to—"

She grabbed his forearm again. "No, please. You were being a perfect gentleman by coming to my defense. And I appreciate it ever so much. Now, let's call the matter settled, shall we?"

He nodded as he replaced his fedora onto his head. "Matter settled. Now let's hope my chivalry doesn't get me into any more trouble."

"Or my pride." She laughed while tossing her head back.

And Titus's heart sailed out to sea.

~

*A*melia tried not to look, but she kept returning her gaze to Titus's eyes, which reflected the glassy sea.

How did the bay resemble a mirror? Or was it silver? Or melted iron ore? Dark and still, except for the waves their boat created, it held secrets of pirates and soldiers, of treasure and of death.

Did the open sea past the peninsula look the same? She'd been to the Atlantic but had only seen oil paintings of the gulf waters. Were the waves truly like lace?

Was the water like emeralds, as the paintings had portrayed?

Either way, Amelia couldn't wait to see the beach that faced the open ocean and feel the gusts against her dress. Would the winds be as strong on this side as they sometimes were on the Atlantic? So strong that one must brace against something to keep from falling over?

Amelia giggled. Would she mind if she had to brace against a fellow passenger?

Not if that someone was Titus Overton.

Another smile danced across her lips, warring with her heart's warning.

"Look!" Titus nudged her with his elbow as he pointed westward into the morning light. "Dolphins!"

"Where?" Amelia shaded her eyes with her right hand, leaning her left hand on the railing, keeping her arm close to Titus's. She squinted in the brightness and focused on the direction in which he pointed. The red and pink flowers on her hat, along with the numerous white goose feathers, made it one of her favorite hats. It suited this dress—and the dress suited her figure—but didn't offer much shade.

"There! Keep watching. They dip down and then they come back up farther down current."

Amelia kept watching, trying to be patient. Maybe if Titus would offer his binoculars, she could see them. "I don't see—oh! I see!" She bounced on her toes. "I see them. They're so beautiful."

Pivoting, she called against the breeze to Goldie and Mae, "Come, watch the dolphins!"

The girls ran to her side, followed by Stanley and then Willis, who had only joined them a few times on their morning walks. When a fifth child joined them, one she didn't recognize, she nodded at him, then focused back out to the bay.

"Where?" Stanley called.

"I don't see dolphins." Mae shaded her eyes with her hands and squinted.

"They're gone!" Willis slumped.

Amelia patted Willis on the back. "No, no, they're still there. Keep watching. They go under to feed, then come back up for air."

Titus pointed again, this time in the southwest direction. "There they are!"

They all ran to Titus's left side and focused their attention until squeals and shouts from all but the newcomer indicated they'd spotted the gray mammals.

"I don't see them. It's too bright. How do I know you're telling the truth? Whatever you think you're seeing is probably a shark, not a dolphin."

This naysayer fifth child had drained Amelia of her exuberance in less than a minute. What was wrong with him?

While she wanted to chastise him, to ask him where his sense of adventure was, to inquire about his need to ruin everyone's fun, something hitched in her gut. Something told her to practice patience. He'd wanted to come along for a reason. Whatever that reason, he needed time to find it.

Releasing a sigh, Amelia spoke, only as loud as she needed to for him to hear her voice over the roar of the engine. "What's your name? I don't believe we've had the pleasure to meet yet."

Arms braced against the railing, he gave his body a heave strong enough to capsize the boat, keeping his gaze focused on the bay. He might not see the dolphins, but his desire to believe etched itself across his face. "Jimmy."

Jimmy? The same Jimmy who had haphazardly almost cost her her time in Point Clear?

He wasn't one of her usual companions. Why had he come today?

Despite the edge of resentment that formed around her heart, Amelia relaxed her shoulders and leaned closer to him. Kindness begat kindness, didn't it? "Jimmy, I'm Miss Harris. The dolphins are out there, even if you can't see them. They swim with many other fish and creatures we don't see. I'm confident that before we return this afternoon to the resort, you'll have seen quite a number of exciting sights, even if the dolphins don't make an appearance again."

He shuffled his shoes on the decking while adjusting his hat. "I want to see the dolphins because the others saw them. It doesn't matter what else I see. If I don't see the dolphins, I'll—"

"Jimmy..." Amelia's voice carried a little more

authority than she'd intended, but if he'd come today to learn about photography, then she was, by all rights, his leader. "We still have the day ahead of us. Let's not allow a sour disposition to ruin everyone else's time, shall we?"

He shifted his gaze toward hers and glared at her. "You're not my mother or my governess. You're not my teacher. You can't speak to me that way."

Amelia stood to her full height, which was but a few inches taller than the lad, who must be nearing fifteen years old. Turning her head and returning her gaze to the bay, she tilted her chin upward. This fellow was obviously not accustomed to taking correction from someone he considered beneath him. If only he'd joined the others with Titus, where they now stood on the other side of the boat.

She spoke over the engine and the wind. "If you don't want to follow my instructions, then you don't have to remain with me. Mr. Overton is your chaperone for the day. Feel free to join him."

After grasping her camera case handle, she pivoted away. Jimmy wasn't her responsibility, and she refused to waste another moment trying to console or direct him.

"Don't walk away from me. Do you know who my father is?"

Amelia kept walking. She'd find a place at the front of the boat where the mist would cool her increasing temper down. She had made too many advancements in her life and taken too many strides toward deserving respect for this. A mere child would not threaten her, no matter who his father was.

She took only a few more steps, passing several passengers who sat on benches which lined the interior cabin, when fire shot through her hand and up her arm to her shoulder.

As Jimmy ran past her as if a sea monster chased him, reality slapped her in the face. Jimmy had snatched her case and now fled with her most valuable asset—an asset that belonged to her employer.

Why did her feet remain frozen to the decking?

She couldn't move.

She couldn't even—

"Titus!"

CHAPTER 7

*A*melia's shriek pierced Titus like the sharpest double-edged sword. Higher pitched than a gull's call, it alerted him to trouble on the opposite side of the boat, reaching to the depths of his soul—because it hadn't been a shriek at all. Amelia had screamed his name. She had chosen him and no one else to come to her aid.

With bile choking him and what felt like octopus tentacles wrapped around his legs impeding each step, he trudged his way through the crowd that had gathered around Amelia.

"Excuse me. Pardon me." Titus used both hands to swim through the sea of people. "Move!"

Other than an ashen face and slumped shoulders, she appeared well—except for her blank stare out to sea and agape mouth. Something had provoked her panic.

"What's wrong? Miss Harris—Amelia, what happened?"

"She's been standing there like that since she screamed," a woman behind him declared. "Are you Titus?"

Keeping his focus on Amelia, he answered, "I am." Then, grasping her shoulders, he shook her petite frame. "Amelia, what's the matter?"

At a snail's pace, she slid her gaze to his as her mouth shut. But when tears flooded her eyes and her brow crumpled, she pulled away from him and bolted toward the front of the boat.

Following her, Titus scanned his surroundings for any signs of danger.

What could have caused the outburst from Amelia and the subsequent shock she'd displayed?

Balancing against the rocking of the boat, Titus continued to chase her.

Would she keep running around and around the interior cabin until she reached whatever she chased or came to a point of exhaustion—whichever occurred first? Was she having some sort of madness due to sun exposure? He'd never seen anything like this. Had it been anyone but her, he'd have called Mack and let him attend to her needs.

"Excuse me. Excuse me. Please clear the way!" Titus kept up his pursuit although Amelia remained out of reach on her second trip around the cabin.

But then she halted a few feet from the railing at the back of the boat.

His gaze moved to what must have caused her hysteria.

No, not what.

Who.

It was a *who* that had caused her to put aside social conventions and propriety in pursuit of her mission.

The boy who had stayed with Amelia when the other children had joined him for the dolphin scouting leaned with his back against the railing. In his right hand, he dangled Amelia's camera case over the water.

Titus closed the distance between them until he stood between Amelia and the boy, heat coursing through his veins and drowning out every sound but her cries for help.

"Jimmy, please, give it back to me! Please!"

Jimmy. Who was this obnoxious fellow who taunted Amelia with a threat that held devastating consequences? Did he not know her camera was more than a hobby piece? Didn't he know that as a photographer, her camera meant everything to her? If he'd spent much time at all with her over the last two weeks, he had to know its importance.

"Jimmy, return Miss Harris's camera to her at once!" Titus took a step toward him.

"Stay there, Mr. This is none of your concern." Jimmy cackled, throwing his head back and wiggling the case over the water.

"This is most definitely my concern, young man. I am your chaperone on this tour."

"You're not my chaperone. My parents don't even know I'm on this boat."

Amelia gasped from her place behind him, sending prickles across Titus's neck. "You came without permission?"

"Well, no matter. You're here. As general manager of the resort, anything that involves our guests concerns me."

When the boat slowed to a stop, Titus widened his stance to steady himself, then locked his knees.

Jimmy stumbled sideways, causing his hold to loosen on the case handle. Then he grasped it with his left hand while keeping his back to the railing and his gaze trained on Titus.

What Jimmy could not see was the panic that streaked across his own face, although he must've felt it rush through his body.

Why panic? If he wanted to drop the case overboard, he could've already done it. He most certainly would have let it go when the boat stalled. So he didn't really want to dispose of Amelia's property. Then what game was he playing here?

Amelia brushed past Titus. "Jimmy, give me my camera. I don't know why you're doing this, but I want to understand. Give me the camera and we can talk." She held out both hands toward Jimmy.

"Stay there! I'll drop it."

"What do you want?" Amelia pleaded, hands still out in front of her as she stepped closer to him.

Titus could tackle the boy in one swift move. But if he did, Jimmy would drop the case into the water. While the bay was no deeper than twelve feet at this spot, the water would ruin the camera before they could dive to retrieve it.

But Titus would try.

He'd try whatever he had to for Amelia.

"Young man—"

Amelia's hand halted Titus's command. He bit back the urge to continue. He'd learned his lesson about intervening. She may have called him in her initial moment of need, but she'd regained her composure and her fortitude and didn't need him now.

He'd stay right here, anyway.

Just in case.

"What's happening here?" Mack Duncan sidled up to Titus's right side.

"One of Miss Harris's protégées has taken possession of her camera for an unknown reason and is threatening to throw it overboard."

Mack leaned closer to Titus. "That's Lloyd Sherwood's boy. Best just let him have the camera. Miss Harris can replace it. The expensive repercussions for any harm that comes to this boy would be far worse than a lost piece of equipment."

Titus jerked his gaze away from the scene which played out in front of him, and facing Mack, glared at him. "So we're supposed to let Sherwood's son do whatever he wants at the expense of an innocent guest? An unaccompanied woman, at that? I will not stand idly by and watch a bully who has unrealistic needs for attention harm Miss Harris, her equipment, or anything or anyone else under my care."

"That's not wise, Titus."

Titus bit back the words he wanted to say, words that would be quite unbecoming of a gentleman. But his anger threatened to explode out his ears if he didn't say or do something.

Jamming his forefinger into Mack's chest, he leaned close enough to him that the tips of their noses almost touched. "You can choose to empower these moguls in their attempts to lord their wealth and supposed supremacy over us, over the ones who serve them, but I will do no such thing."

Mack stepped back, dark eyes glistening in the sun. Was that fear? "Titus, you forget that that's a child standing there. Not another man. A child. A child with a powerful father. If we don't do everything we can to protect him, we—"

Titus snorted. Did Mack even hear himself? He would really let a woman suffer the consequences of a bully's actions? "Then you see to the child—who is nearly a grown man, by the way—and I'll see to Miss Harris." He pivoted toward Amelia and Jimmy, who now stood inches apart at the railing.

The crowd had disbanded while he'd debated with

Mack. Had no one offered to help? Had they only crowded around hoping for a tragic event to write their family about on a penny postcard? The penny post-cards that had brought Amelia to the resort in the first place. Why were people so calloused? So inconsiderate?

But perhaps Amelia had declined their offer to help just as she'd declined his.

"My father will have you fired."

"Your father can't hurt me."

Jimmy pulled the case over the railing, adjusted his grip, and then hung it back over the railing on his left side. His hands must both be reaching exhaustion. Would he be able to keep a tight grip on the case much longer?

Titus stepped closer, but Jimmy shook his head at him. "Stay there! If you come closer, I'll—"

"Titus, please! Don't cause him to do something irrational." Amelia glanced over her shoulder at him, then returned her focus to Jimmy.

"More irrational than this?" Titus threw his hands in the air. This woman's pride and stubbornness would cost her her equipment and probably his job because when they returned to the resort, he would give Lloyd Sherwood a healthy dose of chastisement.

"Jimmy, what did I do to offend you?"

"You...you didn't...you wouldn't show me—"

"Wouldn't show you what? The dolphins? So you steal my camera case from me and hold me and my camera hostage? Until when? Until a dolphin shows itself to you?"

She stepped to the railing and grasped Jimmy's right arm. "I can't show you a dolphin any easier than I can make a rainbow appear over the horizon. You want to see a dolphin without practicing patience. You certainly won't see one as long as you continue to carry out this outlandish charade."

Jimmy studied her face. His gaze flashed from her eyes to her mouth and then back again. Then he glanced over his shoulder at the bay.

While his focus was elsewhere, Titus slipped across the deck to the railing, then locked himself in place close enough to Jimmy that he could outstretch his arms and commandeer the case while Amelia consoled him.

Why did she even bother trying to play the sympathizer with this ruffian? He deserved shackles and chains. Not sympathy.

"Jimmy, seeing a dolphin is the least of your worries. If you drop my camera into the bay, then my employer may seek retribution." Amelia's voice remained unruffled.

He shook his head. "I don't care. My father'll pay the cost."

Titus scooted closer. Just another inch or two and he could grab the case.

"Your father can't serve your sentence for you, Jimmy."

"Sentence?"

Amelia nodded, keeping her gaze focused on him, not alerting Jimmy to Titus's proximity. "Yes, you stole my camera. If you don't return it, you'll be penalized."

Jimmy turned his head and glanced over his shoulder at the bay again, then back at Amelia. "You're tricking me. Just like everyone. You can't have the camera back. You either give it to me or I'll drop it."

Titus could grab the case with only a slight stretch. But if Jimmy offered any resistance at all, it could still land in the dark depths of the bay. So long as the knot remained in Titus's gut and the fury raced through his veins, though, he could not play a passive role here. He'd seize the opportunity and bring an end to this game.

Then, as if out of an Edgar Allan Poe poem, a pelican swooped in and landed on the railing beside Amelia, and Jimmy released his grip on the case with a shriek that matched Amelia's cry at the beginning of this ordeal.

~

*A*melia would never forget Titus's heroic moves to save her case for as long as she drew breath into her lungs. She'd never lie in her bed at night with her eyes closed without seeing him as he agilely swooped up the case when Jimmy dropped it in response to the pelican landing on the railing. Titus had dangled like an acrobat by his waist, almost tipping over and falling into the bay, but he'd saved her camera and her livelihood.

He'd done it even though she'd declared she didn't need his help.

Of course, she'd thought she could talk Jimmy out of his threats. She may have done so—eventually. But the pelican had interfered in her quest to solve the problem with no help from anyone, and Titus had acted without a moment's hesitation.

She'd forever be in his debt, and she didn't mind telling him that.

While Mack Duncan escorted Jimmy to the cabin to be kept under his watchful eyes, and the boat turned starboard and headed back to the resort, Titus remained by the railing with his grip so tight on Amelia's case handle his knuckles had turned white. He hated to disappoint the adventurers, but they could not afford to continue their expedition with Jimmy aboard. He couldn't be trusted not to create more havoc.

Amelia strode to him with a smile offering her thankfulness.

Before she could speak, Titus raised the case in front of him and shrugged. "I apologize."

"For what?" She accepted the case, their fingers touching for just a moment during the exchange. Was the heat which raced up her arm from the sun or from contact with Titus's warm flesh through her glove?

"For intervening."

She shook her head and found his gaze with hers. "No, please, don't apologize. I am so grateful for your valor. You've saved so much more—" Her words caught in her throat that now held so much parchedness she couldn't swallow. "You saved so much more than my camera. You risked your safety for me."

The stinging in her eyes revealed the emotion in her heart. She could never repay this man. Nor would he let her if she could.

"And I would do it again, Amelia Harris. I'd do it again a thousand times." He stepped closer to her and pulled her left hand from her case handle. "I'd do it again a million times, even if you didn't want me to."

CHAPTER 8

*A*melia studied Titus's face, the gleam in his eyes, the three lines which occupied his brow. He didn't seem to care if she knew of his concern for her. Concern was all this was, though, right? As general manager, he needed to ensure his guests' safety and well-being, especially while away from the resort.

Had they been at the resort, would he have intervened?

Amelia lowered her gaze to their hands. Despite the satin gloves, his warmth still reached her skin and invaded her heart. But she'd treat herself well not to let Titus's momentary chivalry fool her into thinking this was anything other than that. He had turned away from her before, and he'd probably do it again.

Raising her gaze to meet his once more, she slid her hand from his, picked up her case, and then leaned against the railing. After placing the case between her skirt and the wall of the boat, she arched her right eyebrow and quirked the left corner of her mouth.

What could she say to relieve him from the vow he'd just declared? She should say something because, otherwise, he might feel compelled to imprison himself with a promise he didn't mean, and that would leave her beholden to him.

Neither one of them needed such an entanglement.

He stepped closer to her, with a flicker of something that looked like genuine interest filling his eyes. "You were going to say?"

She shook her head. "No, I wasn't...I, uh, well—"

"Don't. You don't have to say anything. I'm afraid I've made a fool of myself blubbering over you when you have stated you don't need help. I let my—"

"Titus, please. Don't ever apologize again for coming to my aid. I said I appreciate your help, and I meant it. And while I appreciate your offer to do it again a million times over, I pray that won't be necessary. For if my essentials cause a ruckus like this again—even once more—I'm afraid neither of us would survive it."

He chuckled, and his brow relaxed. His smile, while hidden beneath his mustache, reached his eyes.

"Besides, I wouldn't want you to feel obligated to...I am only one of many guests. You can't rescue every one of us a million times."

He shuffled his feet as the crinkles returned to his brow. "I wouldn't even dare." Grasping the railing, he leaned against it and pointed his gaze to the bay. Soon, they'd be at the resort again, and Titus would resume dodging her. Wouldn't he?

"You wouldn't dare...what?" She had to know what he meant by that declaration.

"I wouldn't dare rescue anyone else a million times or even a thousand." Against the wind, his words almost soared out to sea before they danced across her ears.

Almost.

He faced her, and the sincerity in his voice had stained his cheeks, had moistened his eyes again.

"Or even one hundred times." He swallowed, never moving his gaze from hers.

She tried to swallow, but her mouth held no moisture.

"Only for you."

As her heart thrashed against her ribs and her blood pounded out a staccato rhythm in her neck, she tried to make sense of what he was saying.

What *was* he saying?

Did he mean he held her in a higher regard than he held the other guests? If so, why? If so, then why had he turned away from her when he'd seen her running in the rain?

"I—I don't—I don't understand. Only for me? Why me?"

Heaving a sigh which rivaled the breeze, his shoulders slumped. "Amelia, I do not enjoy making a fool of myself, but when it comes to you, that's exactly what I become."

"Pardon me? I still don't understand." She made him a fool? Not exactly the most flattering accusation.

"When you're near me, things awaken in me that I've long kept sedated. I've done my best to avoid you so this awakening wouldn't happen. But I fear it has, and even when you are out of sight, you remain in my thoughts. I'm very sorry for this and any troubles this may have caused you."

Amelia's heart raced even harder. Tears formed in her eyes, but she blinked them away. Would that their moisture could reach her mouth and unstick her tongue from its roof.

"I'll do my best to stay out of your company when we return to the resort because I know you didn't come here looking for anything but subjects to photograph." He cleared his throat and released his hold on the railing. "The next ten weeks will be torturous for me, but I'll do my best. I must. My heart cannot survive another—"

"Miss Amelia! There you are. Are you all right?" Mae yelled as she ran to her with Goldie and Stanley trailing behind her. "We were so worried Jimmy hurt you."

Amelia pulled her gaze away from Titus's, his declaration still ringing in her ears. Had he just... What had he meant by...

"Miss Amelia?" Mae tugged on her arm.

Focusing on Mae as Titus slipped away, Amelia nodded. "Yes, I am well. My camera is well. Jimmy didn't hurt either of us. I only hate we're returning to the resort and won't see the fort today."

But that wasn't all she hated. She hated that Titus would undoubtedly avoid her for the rest of her stay. She might never know what it could've meant to…

Swallowing down the remorse, she forced her thoughts to focus on the children. They were the perfect distraction.

Titus had said she made a fool of him, and he wouldn't allow it again.

She couldn't permit her heart to fall for anyone this summer, but especially not for a man who behaved so unpredictably, who baffled her with his actions.

~

Titus had done his best these last few weeks to focus on his work—work he didn't enjoy —to keep Amelia out of his thoughts, to forget how he'd embarrassed himself while doting on her on the boat that day. Somehow, she had taken the place in his mind that his beloved birds had held for so long. He'd used the study of his feathered friends to give him hope for a brighter day at the end of summer when he could leave his responsibilities here. Now he had no distraction from the drudgery of managing the resort. Nothing to keep him from remembering the hole Evelyn had left in his life and that Amelia could fill it.

If he could find a suitable replacement from among his current staff, he'd give the man the position and leave today. He'd throw all his efforts and strengths back into the birds and leave this place. He'd travel to the Cayman Islands and get as far away as he could from Amelia Harris and the sludge she dredged out of his heart.

"Mr. Overton, how many campfires will we need on the beach tonight?" Silas Baker's question brought him back to his duties. He might as well focus all his attention on tonight's Independence Day celebration. Maybe the festivities would keep him occupied.

Titus gave Silas a whack on the back as he pasted on a smile. Something he did a lot of these days. "I believe we'll only need four this year. Since two families left this week, and the four new families that will be joining us don't arrive for two days, that leaves us with thirty guests. Four should suffice for the guests plus our staff."

Silas smiled, his dark eyes glowing in the morning light. "We get to partake in the celebration?"

"Of course!" Titus scrubbed his chin and chewed on the details he'd gone over last night. "But Silas, place three of the fires on the south side of the boardwalk and one on the north."

"Yes, sir. Any reason for the separation?"

Releasing a sigh, Titus pulled his gaze away from Silas and scanned the beach area. There was no good way to explain without causing him hurt, so he'd have to say it as gently as he could.

"This is your first summer here, correct?"

"Yes, sir. Came all the way from New Orleans."

"As I thought. You see, Silas, the guests tend to prefer a separation between themselves and the staff. So the three fires for them will be on the south side, and the one for the staff on the north. The south side for them so the gulf breeze will blow past them, driving the smoke from their fires north." Titus turned his gaze on him again.

Silas shook his head, the glimmer in his eyes disappearing. "Their smoke blowing on us instead of ours on them?"

"Precisely." He shrugged. "Of course, the staff is welcome to celebrate elsewhere, on the other side of the point, if this arrangement is too demeaning. I feel certain that would be my choice if I weren't management."

Silas shook his head again. "And make things comfortable for our already-too-comfortable guests? No, sir. I look forward to celebrating downwind from them." A chuckle erupted from him that spread to Titus.

"I like your spirit, Silas."

"Thank you, sir. I'll get to work now."

As Silas strode away, Titus headed for the end of the boardwalk. While he'd given explicit instructions to all guests that there would be no fireworks, no cannons, and no pistol-firing tonight due to the sensitive nature of the nesting birds—and because of the fire that had almost destroyed the east wing of the guests' quarters last year—he didn't fully expect that the night would remain absent of such. Little boys almost always went against the rules, especially when it involved fire or something explosive.

However, while Titus remained general manager, he wouldn't approve of such things by the guests. Only authorized staff could handle explosives under strict supervision. Due to the lack of rainfall the last two weeks, he could not allow it. He'd rather have dissatisfied guests than dead or injured ones.

At the end of the boardwalk, Titus faced south, the morning sun already rising high in the sky and burning away the overnight cloud cover. Across the bay, Bon Secour and Gasque said their morning greetings. What he wouldn't give to charter a sailboat for the day and sail along the shoreline—or straight across the bay.

As he stared across the shimmering water, a rock settled in his gut and soured his appetite for breakfast. His shoulders slumped, and even when he pushed against the wind, they remained slack. What was this heaviness that bore down on him?

Mullet popped out of the water attracting the gulls, but Titus didn't have his usual smile to offer them. He could send them a pretend one, of course, but it would be just that. Counterfeit and without exuberance behind it.

Removing his hat, he extracted his handkerchief from his pocket and swiped his forehead. The millstone stayed with him. He'd never been good at wiping away the troubles that brewed inside him. Sure, he could push them to his core for a while, but they always crept up again.

If he could just—

Something squeezed in his heart and refused to release him. His losses and his circumstances had caused his sour mood. And being stuck here for two more months didn't help. That's all. That's why he was so miserable. Right?

Titus groaned, shoving his handkerchief back into his pocket and jamming his hat into place. He faced west, and although his gaze landed on a school of dolphins slipping across the bay, his brow remained set in the scowl that had made itself home there the last few weeks.

He couldn't blame his circumstances. It wasn't Evelyn's memory that haunted him. It wasn't his desire to leave this place. It wasn't even Amelia Harris. Something—no, someone—seized his mind and held his heart captive.

"Is it you, God? Are You real? Are You why I'm so unsettled?" Titus whispered against the wind as he shoved his hands into his pockets and gripped the cotton's coolness. "Is it Your jealousy that keeping knocking at my heart's door?" Titus gripped his thighs while his hands remained inside his pockets.

I want freedom. I want independence from the struggles that won't let me go.

A warm gust pushed against Titus and blew his hat off his head. Closing his eyes and allowing the warmth to flood his body, he sucked in the salty breeze.

"If that's You, God, if You're offering, I accept. I need freedom."

He didn't really even know what that meant. But he knew he needed it.

Opening his eyes, then bending to retrieve his hat off the boardwalk, Titus blinked away the tears that had spilled from his soul. He glanced over his right shoulder. No one else occupied the space with him. No one had heard him talking out loud to himself —to God.

He popped his hat onto his head and smiled. He'd talked to God? *The* God? Had He heard him?

Titus raised his gaze to the cloudless sky. How could it be possible that the God of the heavens had heard him? The minister had said something about Him being all-present and all-knowing, but Titus still didn't understand.

Yet, after that gust of warmth, something felt lighter in him. The rock no longer sat at the bottom of his stomach.

Was this peace? Was this what he'd been searching for? He'd been so angry with God since he'd lost Evelyn, had denied that God even existed. Why would He listen to him?

And yet it felt as if He had. As if the Creator of the world had welcomed him home.

Titus pivoted toward the shoreline. He had to tell someone. He couldn't keep this newfound freedom to himself. Who could he share it with?

The only person he wanted to let into this private corner of his life, he'd successfully managed to forever repel.

But still...

Titus pushed past the cluster of guests who had gravitated to the end of the boardwalk and headed to the dining hall on a quest to find Amelia.

"Mr. Overton, a word, please." Lloyd Sherwood's booming voice coming from the direction of the pavilion halted Titus in his path and threatened to rip his joy right from him.

With a sigh, Titus headed to Sherwood, forbidding his forehead to draw into a knot. He'd smile. Sherwood didn't have to know who put the smile on his face. "Good morning. What can I do for you?"

Stubble graced Sherwood's upper lip and his cheeks. Had he decided to join the majority of the men here at the resort in the end-of-summer beard competition?

Titus chuckled inside, fighting his urge to laugh out loud. Sherwood might need to return next year for the competition because he hardly seemed capable of growing facial hair at any pace, much less a quick one.

"My son wants to participate in the celebration

tonight without being chaperoned by his mother or myself. He's complied with your requirements since the *incident* on the boat. I've talked to the board of directors and let them know how unfair I feel your punishment was against the boy, who was only playing a harmless prank. So I expect you to mark his period of segregation as done and allow him to return to his summer activities." Sherwood's ruddy cheeks and nose contrasted the whites of his eyes and left no room for misunderstanding. He wasn't asking.

He *expected*?

Titus folded his arms across his middle, widening his stance. As much as he desired to keep Jimmy under the constant supervision of his parents, he'd served his punishment without causing any ripples around the resort. Titus should extend grace to him, allow him to experience freedom. Wasn't that the purpose of today?

Heaving another sigh, Titus nodded. "Very well. But know he will remain the subject of my caution. And I advise that he keep his distance from Miss Harris. His prank wasn't as harmless as you suggest and caused her great anxiety."

Sherwood squinted at Titus but remained where he stood. "Some people shouldn't insert themselves into places they don't belong if they aren't sturdy enough to manage a prank or two, especially one from a mere boy."

Titus dropped his arms to his sides, balling his

hands into fists. If Sherwood gave him one more reason, he might take him down right here and now.

No. Resist. There is a better way.

"All I'm saying is that a tenderhearted woman who can't find humor in a prank perhaps should stay with the other delicate flowers."

"Good day, Mr. Sherwood." Titus spun away from him before he did or said anything to ruin his reputation as a gentleman.

But if the Lord provided a way to humble Sherwood, Titus wouldn't mind one single bit.

CHAPTER 9

*A*melia exited the dining hall, still licking the maple syrup off her lips, although making sure no one saw her do it. What should she photograph today?

Some days, it seemed as though she'd already photographed everything she could and that a full summer here wasn't necessary. Then the next day, an unfamiliar flower blossomed or the wind rustled through the Spanish moss in a different direction than the day before and gave the oaks to which it clung a fresh look. They begged for her to photograph them.

As guests who were once strangers became friends after several weeks at the resort, the photographs Amelia took of them held more life. Frolicking in the bay, sailing in sailboats, having picnics beneath the ancient oaks—these pals posed for Amelia with more vibrancy than when they'd first arrived. Many approached her requesting her services instead of her asking them.

Tomorrow, she might have to bring her camera to breakfast and request permission to capture the chefs while cooking. She'd been here more than a month, and not a day had gone by that something on the menu hadn't surprised her. If only her camera could capture the vibrant colors the chefs brought into each dish. Whether it was the spices or the various fruits and vegetables, food here at the resort seemed almost too visibly pleasing to eat. But she didn't let the beauty stop her from indulging.

The cakes and pastries weren't as colorful as many of the ones Amelia had seen back home or in New York City, but the lead chef, Chef François Bougère from New Orleans, had told her that was because he refused to put any artificial or potentially toxic coloring in his foods.

"Only the best for the resort guests," he'd said with a wink. While she'd photographed him, the dark-skinned man with wiry hair poking out from beneath his chef's hat had shared with her how he'd come to the resort.

After losing his entire family to yellow fever two months earlier, he'd landed here for a new start. But he carried with him his mother's love for cooking and said that was why the smile stayed on his face even though his heart still ached from his losses. Amelia couldn't help but wonder if his glow came from his liberal use of cayenne pepper.

As she followed the path from the dining hall back to her quarters, her thoughts returned to one subject she'd still been unable to capture—and probably never would.

Titus.

He'd never scheduled his appointment for his portrait. Although the board of directors made sure all other staff had appeared before her camera, Titus hadn't interacted with her since their morning on the boat together. And while Amelia understood that the connection they'd shared was fleeting and would never return, if only it didn't have to be so. It was for the best, though, so Titus wouldn't feel foolish.

She'd forfeit all her photographing opportunities for the rest of the summer just to have one session with the man whose eyes gleamed like twilight, whose features might as well have been chiseled out of Italian marble.

"Excuse me, miss." Someone tapped her shoulder.

When she pivoted and faced the intruder of her thoughts, a small auburn-haired man barely an inch taller than her stood on the path.

"Yes?" She tried not to look cross with him for disrupting her.

"You were standing like a statue there, miss. Are you all right?"

She giggled and stepped aside. "Please pardon my rudeness. I was lost in my thoughts."

He nodded and went on his way.

Amelia brushed a stray wisp of hair from her face. If only she could let her hair down and have the salty breeze blow through it. Maybe if she could sneak away to a private spot somewhere, she'd do just that.

As a cluster of guests strolled past her, the men tipped their hats and nodded while the women either smiled or waved.

She returned their smiles even though something like a dark cloud settled on her heart. Where was her pod? Her group of friends? She didn't even have that back home. Her evenings were spent with Aunt Patsy and Aunt Polly cross-stitching or knitting, talking about a future that felt like it would never come.

Amelia relaxed her lips, letting her artificial smile fade from her face.

Where was her special someone? If he was in Philadelphia, they'd somehow missed each other so far. Her aunts had said maybe he wasn't ready for her yet. Maybe he was still at university. Maybe he...

Maybe he had already died a tragic death, and they'd never meet now.

No, don't think that way. If you act defeated, then you are defeated.

Straightening her shoulders and pulling her chin up, Amelia pivoted and stepped back onto the path. She'd join the game of croquet they'd announced at breakfast, and she'd play this time, not photograph. She needed some time to feel like a guest instead of a commissioned worker.

When her gaze landed on Titus, marching toward her with a scowl on his face, arms swinging by his sides like a soldier's, she halted.

What had she done wrong now?

Even with his eyebrows knotted at the bridge of his nose and his frown peeking out from under his mustache, his approaching presence provoked her heart into beating quicker than normal, brought a tremble to her legs that her dress hid, thankfully.

Keeping her shoulders pressed against the thick morning breeze, she smiled and tried not to let her worry nor her captivation show on her face.

Titus reached her and pulled to a full stop a foot from her, the fragrance of his barber's soap wafting across her nose in the breeze and filling her with the delight of citrus and lavender. "Amelia, I must speak with you this instant." He grasped her elbow, his hand's warmth radiating through her cotton sleeve and up her arm.

"Of course. Have I done something to—"

"No, no, not at all." Titus led her off the path and to an oak tree beside the tables that had been set up for lunch.

"You seemed flustered. I assumed..." Why did she always assume the worst? Why did she always think everyone's ill mood was a result of her actions?

Titus released her elbow but remained close. "I'm sorry for that. I should have done better to hide my mood. I had been in quite a favorable mood and needed to share the reason why with someone. You were the one that came to mind. However, Sherwood stopped me before I could get to you and soured that good mood."

Amelia tilted her head so the brim of her hat would block out the sun and give her a better view of Titus's face, which now seemed relieved of the scowl. "Please, tell me all of it. I want to hear what provoked you to come find me, and I want to hear what Mr. Sherwood said that robbed you of your joy."

A chuckle burst from Titus, then he bit his bottom lip as he scanned their surroundings. How sad that he didn't feel the freedom to express his emotions.

"You laugh because...?"

Titus clasped his hands in front of him, shoulders relaxed again. "Joy. You said *joy*. It's been the ivory-billed woodpecker of my life. I've searched for it even when I didn't know I was searching, but I've never found it. Yet I found it less than ten minutes ago at the end of the boardwalk." He sucked in a breath, then exhaled. "And you were the first person I wanted to tell."

Amelia's heart did a somersault, and a smile broke out on her face that she couldn't contain if she tried. Judging from the breath that inflated his chest, the rest of the story was about to pop out of him. Still, she had to ask. "Joy found at the end of the boardwalk, you say?

I must know about this! But first, why did you lose it on your way to find me?"

"Sherwood stopped me and wanted to talk about his son's punishment. He said some things that made me want to act in an ungentlemanly way. My joy sailed out to sea in that moment. And then…"

Amelia clasped his left forearm and stared up into his face. "What happened?"

"And then I had a thought about him that made me realize how depraved I truly am and that I don't deserve joy."

Amelia's head began shaking in contradiction before Titus finished his sentence. She pulled him over to one of the tables, then waved her left hand toward the bench. "Sit. Let's discuss this. I'm sure you're wrong, for I do not see a man who's undeserving of joy. I see a man who's kind and caring, especially for wildlife, a man who has great responsibility stacked upon his shoulders and who needs joy. So tell me first, this joy you found at the end of the boardwalk, what was it? A sighting of something you've looked for? Or—"

"It was freedom. It was…it was your God. He found me." Tears welled up in Titus's eyes, and he didn't bother wiping them away.

Amelia's eyes filled with tears too. What a happy day of independence for Titus! "That's wonderful, Titus. Simply wonderful!"

"Yes, but—"

"No, no *buts*. You found the love and freedom God

has to offer you. You belong to Him now. Nothing can take that away from you." She patted his hand where it rested on the table. "Even when someone does something to sour your mood, you're still God's child. Even if you act upon your ill thoughts, as we so often do, you're still His."

"Don't I need to follow some laws or rules or—"

"Titus, you will have a lifetime to build your commitment to God. As you spend time reading the Scriptures—" She gasped. "You need a Bible!" Then she grinned. This was the most fantastic of days! Clearing her throat, she patted his hand again.

When he turned his hand over and clasped hers, her heart skipped a beat.

She had better finish her thought before she did something unladylike like grab him in an embrace. Squeezing his hand, she locked gazes with him. "As I was saying, you will have the rest of your life to build a relationship with God. As you read the Scriptures and surround yourself with people who believe in Him, you'll grow and become more like Him."

"But where do I start?"

"Sunday, come to service with me. Then afterward, perhaps we could spend some time reading about God's son, Jesus, and what He did so you could have this freedom and joy you found today."

Titus nodded. "Jesus. Yes, the minister spoke of Him. I remember someone talking about Him when I was a child. I think that's who I found. But why did my mood sour so quickly afterward? Isn't joy supposed to be forever?"

Squeezing his hand once more, Amelia scooted an inch closer to him. "Joy and peace are not found in our circumstances. They're different from feeling happy. At any time, we can become sad or angry or happy or— well, anything. But the joy you find in Jesus will still be there. It might take a while for you to feel better when something sours your mood, but that's okay. Be patient. Especially, be patient with yourself."

Titus gave her hand a squeeze, then released it. "Thank you. I pride myself on being knowledgeable, and if I'm perfectly honest, I'm not sure I take a fancy to being unknowledgeable about this."

"We all must begin somewhere. I was brought up attending services every week. My father read the Scriptures to us every night before bed. But still, I had to find my own faith in God. We are children of God, not grandchildren."

Titus arched his right eyebrow. "I don't—"

"This means that even if all the generations before us believed in Jesus, our security in the family of God comes only when we personally choose to accept Him."

"Ah, so no inheritance without being a child."

She laughed. "Exactly! And you are now a child of God." Clapping, she didn't even try to suppress her giggle.

"That brings me great joy. Thank you for sharing this moment with me."

"Yes, my pleasure."

Titus stood and offered his hand to help her to her feet.

As she accepted it and stood, she gazed up at him. "I suppose you have a full day today."

"Only filled with making sure the guests are satisfied."

"Only..." She smiled.

"I'm afraid it's a job that is not easily done. What's on your itinerary for the day?"

"I considered setting up my darkroom, but it is a celebration day, so I may play some games and take a dip in the bay. Perhaps take my Brownie around and capture the festivities."

Titus nodded, releasing her hand. "I do recall, I offered to help you with your darkroom. I'm happy to do so after lunch, if you'd—"

An explosion interrupted Titus and knocked them back onto the benches, screams filling the morning air.

Titus covered Amelia's body with his. The weight of him pressed the air out of her lungs. Was he dead? Had the explosion killed him before he'd had the chance to see how good a life with the Lord could be?

CHAPTER 10

S creams. Cries. Wails from every direction. Footsteps pounding the earth around Titus. The stench of sulfur assaulted his nostrils, robbed him of his very breath.

When a coughing spasm overtook him, he pushed off the softness beneath him and allowed his lungs a chance to bring fresh air to his body. Although, the air was filled with smoke and wasn't fresh at all.

Titus coughed again as he wiped his stinging eyes.

As guests scattered like mice and cockroaches when one turned on the kitchen lamps in the middle of the night, Titus's gaze fell on the object of everyone's fear.

The shed.

Still in flames, the building that housed their supplies, unused equipment, and chemicals billowed with caustic smoke in shades of black and gray.

Where was his staff with the water cart? They

should have already begun dowsing the flames with the water stored in the tank. They'd practiced for something like this all spring before guests arrived.

Titus lurched forward toward the main building, but when the debris of the moment cleared from his thoughts, he halted and pivoted back to where he'd been moments before.

Amelia!

He'd been with Amelia at the tables. She'd been the softness beneath his body.

Staggering as another round of spasms burst from his lungs, his gaze landed on her.

There she sat at the table, her arms encircling three children, her gaze locked on his. He'd abandoned her in his confusion, and she'd become like Florence Nightingale in a moment's passing.

Was there no end to this woman's charity? No boundary of who she cared for and how much?

And yet, something flashed across her face that spoke of her feelings. Coupled with concern for her charges, pain—not fear—crinkled her brow and brought a frown to her lips that normally turned upward.

Titus made his way back to her, shirking his responsibilities to the other guests while studying the face he could look at for a thousand years. What provoked the angst that stained her beauty right now? The blast hadn't distributed any shrapnel this far, for if it had, Titus himself would have injuries.

When tears spilled from her eyes as they shifted to view the shed, then returned to his, understanding gripped his heart and landed like a rock in his gut.

Her chemicals.

Everything she had brought with her for developing her film was gone.

All gone up in flames.

"Amelia, I'm—I don't—don't worry. We will replace what you've lost."

She rose from the bench while releasing her embrace on the children. "Run along and find your mothers. Stay far away from the fire."

Returning her gaze to his, she stepped closer. "Thank you for shielding me."

He nodded, the moisture that had remained in his mouth now gone. "Of course. I didn't even—I'm not sure I—"

"Titus, you acted very heroically even if you weren't aware of it. You did so because you care about people."

"I would've done whatever I needed to for you to stay safe, Amelia."

No, no, no, don't let your heart do this to you again. You can't love again because you can't lose again.

A cackle from behind Amelia dragged both of them out of whatever this was that stirred between them again.

Amelia pivoted toward the heinous sneer as Titus found the source of it.

Jimmy Sherwood. Standing there with a live fire-cracker between the meaty fingers of his right hand.

Amelia gasped as she covered her mouth with her hands.

Truth had dawned on her as it had settled like a black cloak around Titus's mind.

Jimmy had set the shed on fire with a firecracker!

Titus bolted toward the monster who stood less than eight feet from Amelia and who could—no, most likely would—throw the lit firecracker at her at any moment.

"Titus!"

Although Amelia called from behind him, he cast all propriety to the wind and closed the distance between him and the boy. After knocking the fire-cracker out of his hand, Titus tackled Jimmy to the ground, biting back the words of repulsion that sat on the end of his tongue. Sweat dripped from him onto Jimmy's back as he pressed his knee into it and held his head to the ground.

"Let me go! My father will—"

The firecracker exploded to the right, followed by more screams from surrounding guests.

Titus's staff rolled the water cart past him, and he nodded his thanks while summoning Felix with a quick jerk of his neck.

"Let me go!"

"Oh, I'll let you go, all right." Titus stood, then yanked Jimmy off the ground, keeping his grasp secured around the boy's wrists. "I'll let you go right into the capable hands of my assistant, who will hold you in his office until arrangements have been made to remove you and your family from the premises. Permanently!"

Jimmy struggled against Titus's hold, but he held tight until Felix joined them and he turned him over to him.

"Felix, see to it he's kept under your watchful eye. Find Lloyd Sherwood and remove the entire family from the resort. Make sure they know the Sherwoods are no longer welcome here."

Felix nodded as he dragged Jimmy away.

"You sure that's necessary?" Amelia's voice floated on the smoky breeze from behind him.

Titus turned and faced her. There it was again. The concern for others, even her enemies.

He pushed his shoulders back while releasing a sigh. "I know you don't want to see anyone hurt, Amelia, but this boy's menacing ways are no longer something we can excuse. He could've killed someone with that explosion. He caused us a great deal of loss with that stunt. He is on a downward spiral and must be stopped before something tragic happens."

"I fear you may have made an enemy, though."

Titus shrugged, even though her words spoke a truth of consequences he might not easily recover from. "So be it if I did. This resort is my responsibility. And the guests are in my care. I will not let one endanger the lives of many, no matter who his father is."

~

Sunrise had seemed a preposterous time when they made the announcement at breakfast yesterday that for the rest of the summer while the temperatures soared, the minister would hold services early on Sunday mornings. But now that Amelia sat in one of the folding chairs among fifty or so others on the brick courtyard facing the bay, the coolness of the breeze blowing across her cheeks, she couldn't begrudge having to get up several hours earlier than normal. Last week's service at ten in the morning had put her and the other fair-skinned guests at risk for sunburn even though they'd all worn hats and gloves. Several of the older folks had complained of the heat and claimed they wouldn't return unless they moved the meeting to an earlier time.

Amelia stifled a giggle as the images of those same folks sitting in canoes and on the end of the boardwalk at high noon the same day danced across her memory. Some people did what they wanted whenever they wanted and found complaining to be an enjoyable pastime. Many of those same people still complained no matter what others did to accommodate them.

That had certainly been the case with Sherwood. While Titus had insisted the entire family be removed from Point Clear, Mr. Kroyer and the board of directors had overruled him. It seemed as though the money Sherwood brought to the resort in referrals alone held more value to the ones in charge than did the safety and comfort of the general population here.

Amelia sighed as she massaged away the crease which formed between her eyebrows.

Lord, could you see fit to give Mr. Sherwood a nudge about leaving? If not, please keep him and his son Jimmy far from me.

"Excuse me, are you saving these seats for anyone?"

Amelia glanced upward against the bright morning to find a cluster of young women barely twenty years old, dressed all in white and smiling at her. Turning her gaze toward the six vacant chairs between her and the LeBlancs at the end, she shook her head, then waved her hand toward them. She counted the women as they each crossed in front of her.

Five of them. That left one vacant chair in case...

Amelia dropped her shoulders while at the same time trying not to let her lack of hope show on her face. She'd never been good at masquerading, but perhaps today she could hide from the other attendees what her heart felt.

After all, she'd come to service this morning to hear a word of encouragement from the minister and to sing a few hymns to lift her spirits.

Just because she hadn't heard from Titus since the explosion—not even after she'd sent him the New

Testament that had belonged to Pa—it didn't mean she wouldn't hear from him. A man like that had too many responsibilities, especially since the incident, to fritter his time away with her. A woman who would leave in a month and a half and never see him again. He was much too important, and she was much better off.

Although...she'd treasure the opportunity to share more about Jesus with him.

"May I?" A light touch warmed her shoulder even as the baritone voice sent shocks of elation to her toes.

Amelia glanced up into Titus's face, his smile spilling out from under his mustache as the sunlight reflected in his eyes.

"Yes, please." Amelia scooted down one seat, giving Titus the chair on the end in case he had to exit the service before it ended.

Besides, she didn't want to share him with any of the young women sitting on the row with her.

"I had hoped to find you here this morning even though the hour is so early." Titus settled into the seat beside her. Yet instead of leaning back, he turned toward her, putting his back to the isle. He leaned his left arm on the back of the chair. Reaching into his suit-coat pocket, he slid out the Bible.

Pa's Bible rested in the hands of a man she barely knew. What would Aunt Polly and Aunt Patsy think of her gesture?

"Thank you for sending this to me. We'll place a new order for supplies at the end of the week, so I'll order one then. It may take until the end of the summer, but I'll return this. And in the meantime, I'll take great care of it."

"You may keep it for as long as you'd like. No need to return it. It's my gift to you."

A blush touched Titus's cheeks as a twinkle danced in his eyes. "But I believe this belonged to your father?"

"It did. But he's gone on now, and he has no use of it. I'm only sorry I didn't have a full Bible to give you." She rubbed her gloved hand across the Bible's black leather cover, which rested on her lap. "Unless you'd like to borrow—"

"Thank you, Amelia, but you've already been too kind and more than generous. I wouldn't be opposed, however, to spending some late afternoons with you reading from yours. Perhaps after the guests have taken their leave for naptime but before the dinner rush begins?"

Now the blush spread to Amelia's cheeks. Or, at least, the flaming of her face felt as though it had. She couldn't blame this on the heat of the day.

"I'd—I'd like that."

The minister stepped to the podium and everyone quieted. "Thank you for joining us this morning. Let us begin by acknowledging our Lord and Creator through song. Please turn in your hymnals to page forty-two and join us in 'All Things Bright and Beautiful.'"

Titus leaned back in his seat as he tucked the Bible into his pocket. Bending toward her, he whispered in her ear. "I'm afraid I'll have to observe. I'm not familiar with the hymns."

Amelia took a second to enjoy the warm tickle that his breath placed on her ear and neck, then whispered back to him. "I think you'll fancy this one." Then she joined the congregation after the refrain.

Each little flower that opens,
Each little bird that sings,
He made their glowing colors,
He made their tiny wings.

All things bright and beautiful,
All creatures great and small,
All things wise and wonderful,
The Lord God made them all.

"*That* was beautiful." Titus whispered into Amelia's ear after the last refrain.

"I thought you'd find it meaningful."

"Today's sermon comes from Matthew chapter six. Let us read verse twenty-six together aloud." The minister opened his Bible.

Amelia helped Titus find the correct page after he retrieved the Bible from his pocket. How wonderful that the minister had chosen something from the New Testament, allowing Titus to join in the congregational reading.

Amelia had sealed this verse in her heart years ago, so instead of opening her Bible, she closed her eyes and recited it from memory, as Titus's voice melded with hers.

"'Behold the fowls of the air: for they sow not, neither do they reap, nor gather into barns; yet your Heavenly Father feedeth them. Are you not much better than they?'"

As the minister delivered the message on the importance of dependence on God, the God who loves, cares for, and provides for his children, Amelia couldn't stop flicking side glances at Titus, who sat with mouth agape the entire time.

The man who had seemed to know it all and to need no one now looked utterly enamored by the attributes of God. Would he now begin to believe he held worth and purpose and that he didn't need to escape to an island populated mainly with birds?

CHAPTER 11

"And so you see..." Amelia closed her Bible on her lap, then folded her lace-covered hands on top of the book. "...the people who witnessed Jesus after He resurrected spread the word about this miracle, and that's how it all started. Although it may seem hard to believe He rose from the dead, there's proof He did."

Titus grinned at Amelia, as he'd done too many times since they'd settled on the bench at the edge of the woods beneath the oaks and pines. "It all seems so impossible to fathom, but people have been telling the story for thousands of years, so I suppose it must be true."

Amelia smiled at him again. She'd already displayed more patience than one deserved in a lifetime. "That's called faith. Believing without seeing. But we have their testimony which verifies the truth of the events surrounding Jesus's life, death, resurrection, and ascension into heaven to be with the Father. And while we can't physically see Jesus, He's with us in spirit and will make Himself known to you in ways that are unique to you. Just keep watching for Him and listening with your heart."

Titus had always needed proof before he believed. When Evelyn died, he refused to accept it until he'd seen her body in the morgue. He couldn't believe the airplane existed until he saw the photograph of the Wright brothers for himself. The same with the Ferris wheel, which he never would have imagined could exist until he'd ridden it himself at the World's Fair in Chicago with Uncle Sidney.

Titus removed his hat and placed it on his lap. After combing his right hand through his hair, he rested both hands atop his hat, lacing his fingers. "Faith. That's challenging. I am a see-it kind of man. However, I felt something that day on the boardwalk I've never felt before. I'll keep that memory in the forefront of my mind from this day forward."

"That's what we all do. Keep remembering. Keep searching. You will find Him." After Amelia's gaze flipped upward to the branches of the magnolia to their left, her face beamed as though she had seen Jesus Himself. Pointing toward the tree, she gasped. "What is that bird? I've never seen anything like it."

Titus reluctantly shifted his gaze, then searched the tree for the bird which had captivated her. It took no more than half a minute to find the brilliant blue contrasting with the deep green of the magnolia leaves. "That's the indigo bunting in all its brilliance. They summer here."

Amelia covered her mouth as she gasped again. "It is magnificent. Absolutely magnificent. How do you know so much about birds?" With glistening eyes, she turned her gaze back to him.

Finding a close match to the bird's feathers in her eyes, Titus focused on them with no reluctance. He could stare at her every hour of the day. "I suppose I've studied birds like you've studied the Scriptures."

She nodded, lowering her hands to her lap. "I'm not sure I've ever met someone as knowledgeable as you."

He chuckled. "I doubt that. I may know birds and other wildlife, how to run a resort, and other sundry things, but you're knowledgeable in ways I am not. And your ability to exhibit kindness, patience, and—"

"Mr. Overton, might I have a word with you?"

Titus jerked his gaze away from Amelia as a scowl settled on his face at the rudeness of the guest who'd interrupted his time with her. Clearing his throat, he stood, then clasped his hands behind his back. "Of course. How may I assist you?"

"I'm Martin Hooper. My family and I have been here over a month. We've reserved our room until the end of July, but we'd like to return home on the next voyage. I believe one is scheduled for tomorrow?"

Titus nodded. "May I inquire about why you want to leave? Are your accommodations unsatisfactory?"

Seldom had guests left before the end of their reserved time unless an emergency called them home.

Mr. Hooper avoided Titus's gaze, focusing on the ground for a few seconds before looking at him again. With deep emotion clouding his dark eyes, he released a heavy sigh. "Our accommodations are more than satisfactory. We enjoy being here. My wife has made many new acquaintances. My daughters never want to leave." Clearing his throat, he shoved his shoulders back. "Well, two of my daughters could stay here permanently. Our eldest daughter, Mary-Elizabeth, now fifteen, wants to leave straightaway."

"I'm sorry to hear this. Is there nothing we can do to make her time here more enjoyable?" Titus glanced over his shoulder at Amelia, then returned his gaze to Mr. Hooper. "Miss Harris, the photographer, has spent a great deal of time with some of the children teaching them about photography. Perhaps—"

"Yes, I'd be more than happy to spend some time with her." Amelia joined them.

Titus smiled at her, then caught a flicker of recognition in her eyes when she looked at Mr. Hooper. Had they met? Had his daughter already spent time with Amelia? The children on the trip to Fort Morgan seemed younger than fifteen.

Mr. Hooper's shoulders slumped and a frown tainted his lips. "I am familiar with Miss Harris."

She nodded but said nothing.

What had transpired between them?

Titus arched his right eyebrow, trying not to let his confusion show. "Would your daughter be disagreeable to spending time with Miss Harris?"

"Sir, she wants to go home, and it has nothing to do with Miss Harris." After shoving his hands into his pants pockets, he continued. "Miss Harris may remember witnessing a disagreement between myself and Lloyd Sherwood one night at dinner."

"I do," she whispered.

"We disagreed over political views, and Sherwood had no qualms about telling me my opinions could get me shunned by society and possibly killed."

Amelia groaned. "I remember it well."

"Our conversation offended you."

"No, sir, it wasn't that. It was Mr. Sherwood's audacity that affronted me. He all but commanded you to adopt his opinions. I agree with yours."

"Thank you."

Titus studied them both for a moment before interjecting. "I'm puzzled by how this has caused your daughter to want to leave."

"Mary-Elizabeth has somehow and against her wishes become the object of Sherwood's son's attention and possibly his affections. I'm not certain if he has a harmless infatuation with her or if it leans toward something a bit more imperiling. But she has informed him multiple times she does not wish to know him, have him court her, or spend any time with him in any capacity. His behavior seems to be escalating, as he has vocalized several times he will have her, and if he can't, no one will. I've spoken with his father, but I'm sure you can imagine that my words fell on deaf ears. Sherwood stated he would never allow his son to associate with my daughter due to my political views, but the taunting has continued. And since the board of directors elected to allow the Sherwood family to stay, I'm afraid my family must go."

The weight pressing down on Titus's shoulders threatened to sink his body into the sandy soil. His position as general manager made it impossible for him to do what he wanted to do in this moment. For if he could, he would toss Sherwood and his family off the resort and give the Hoopers an extra month here free of charge.

Where was the fairness in this? A respected family leaving because a despicable family held too much power? This shouldn't be.

"Mr. Hooper, let me see what I can do. Give me until the morning. If I can't find a solution, I'll refund your money and escort you safely to the boat."

Mr. Hooper nodded but no hope flickered in his eyes. "Till the morning. But I'm not a believer in miracles, so I'll have my family get our things packed away in our trunks." He tipped his hat at Amelia, then pivoted away from them.

"Amelia, I'm afraid I must—"

She held up her hand and stopped his words. "Go.

No need to apologize. This matter is pressing. Go work a miracle." Her smile gave him courage.

Could he stand up to the board and give them an ultimatum? The Sherwoods needed to leave. The resort's reputation depended on it.

~

*A*melia couldn't blame her fitful night on the storm. For while the palms had whacked the hotel all night as the howling winds brought goosebumps over her body, her thoughts had kept her awake. Good families shouldn't feel threatened on their vacations—or ever. Antagonistic boys and their fathers shouldn't have dominion in a place they didn't even own.

Amelia massaged her right shoulder as she sipped her second cup of cocoa from her spot across the table from Martin Hooper's wife, Ruth, and his daughters. She'd come early to breakfast because she'd woken before sunrise and because she'd hoped to secure a spot at the Hooper's table. Maybe her presence could show them she understood their hardship and stood beside them in their quest.

"Mrs. Hooper, I don't believe I've had the pleasure of photographing your family this summer."

Ruth stirred a lump of sugar into her tea and took a sip. After placing her cup onto the porcelain saucer in front of her, she smiled and found Amelia with her sable gaze. "You are quite correct. We'd intended to schedule a time with you, but either Mr. Hooper had a round of golf or our daughters found an activity they preferred more than sitting like a statue for the length of time it would take to capture our images."

Amelia tapped the fingers of her left hand on the table while thumbing her fork with her right. "I understand this may be your last day here. I'd enjoy the opportunity to capture your family with my camera before you go. You'd only need to sit for a few minutes. I'd send the photograph to you once I return home. You see, I had the ability to develop film here, however..." She captured her bottom lip with her teeth as she bit back her words.

Mary-Elizabeth slumped in her spot across the table from Amelia. "Your chemicals exploded when Jimmy Sherwood threw the firecracker at the shed."

"Mary-Elizabeth!" Ruth shot her a stern glance.

"She's correct. The boy did a great deal of damage that day." Amelia's heart squeezed with residual pain, remembering how Jimmy's actions had not only ruined the shed and her supplies but the day's festivities. "I don't mean to gossip about him."

"You aren't gossiping. We all know that's what happened. Now if only their family would leave, we could stay." Ruth took a bite of her biscuit as Mr. Hooper joined them.

Sweat beaded on his tanned brow, which lay etched with lines of worry.

"What did they say, dear?" Ruth placed her hand on his hand.

Amelia smiled at the exchange between the man and woman who must've been married close to twenty years.

"The board decided they should leave and we should stay."

Mr. Hooper's daughters clapped and buzzed with the excitement of bees.

"But..." Mr. Hooper rubbed the lines on his forehead with eyes shut.

"But?" Ruth nudged him with her hand.

"Mr. Hooper, what did they say?" Amelia leaned closer, no longer caring about the melted butter on her biscuit or the savory scrambled eggs beside it.

He opened his eyes and stared across the room. "They received word that more storms are on the way, so they've halted all ferries for the week."

The daughters groaned in unison.

"So I am afraid we must endure our circumstances a bit longer. Sherwood knows to keep his son away from Mary-Elizabeth, or the boy may suffer the consequences of my wrath." Mr. Hooper retrieved his fork and knife, then cut into the ham on his plate with fury.

If Jimmy had any sense in his head, he'd stay away from Mary-Elizabeth.

When Titus joined them at the table, Amelia gulped as her heart tickled her ribs like a feather beneath her nose. No man had ever provoked these responses from her. Not any of the highest men in all of Philadelphia's society nor any of the most common men she'd encountered at church or at social gatherings. If she'd met Titus Overton back home, her aunts wouldn't have had to mention his name or give her any encouragement to accept his calls twice. For if he'd have called, she'd have accepted his company.

While Titus conversed with Mr. Hooper, Amelia tried not to stare at him. But try as she might, her gaze remained locked on the man. How had she let her heart betray her like this? An attraction to a man who she'd never see again once she left at the end of the summer could only break her heart. An infatuation with a man she knew so little about made no sense.

Lord, why have you allowed me to meet him here? Why now? There is no chance of a future with him.

When Titus shifted his gaze from Mr. Hooper to Amelia, then smiled enough that the crinkles around his eyes revealed an inner joy, Amelia dropped her fork, the clank on her plate drawing everyone's attention who sat at the table with her.

Her cheeks must look redder than the strawberry preserves in the dish in front of her, for they burned hot.

Titus, ever the gentleman, diverted focus to himself by clearing his throat. Then, as he patted Mr. Hooper on the shoulder, his brow drew into a knot. "I'm regretful I couldn't resolve your grievances in a more timely manner. But I pray this week passes quicker than a shooting star and you and your family will be back to enjoying your stay here by the week's end."

"I hope so." Mr. Hooper took a sip of his coffee, then sighed.

Amelia felt his turmoil from across the table. One more day with the Sherwood family here could prove challenging. An entire week? Without God, it would be impossible to bear.

"Good day." Then Titus smiled at her. "Miss Harris."

And with that salutation, her heart lifted.

As Titus pivoted away from the table, Sherwood appeared from the far corner of the room, followed by Jimmy, both glaring at Mr. Hooper like angry bulls as they strode in their direction.

Before Amelia could gather her thoughts enough to realize what was happening, Mr. Sherwood reached Mr. Hooper and landed a blow to his face, knocking him out of his chair and onto the floor.

Ruth screamed as she scrambled out of the way.

Mary-Elizabeth let out a wail, drawing Amelia's attention.

Jimmy had latched onto her hair and yanked her out of her chair. Squeezing her against his chest, he glared at Amelia, almost daring her to challenge him. He held Mary-Elizabeth in the same leveraging manner he'd held Amelia's camera case over the boat railing.

Titus returned to the table, joining the men on the floor as punches flew left and right.

When Amelia glanced back at Mary-Elizabeth, her heart sank to her feet.

Jimmy had snatched her out of the room.

Amelia needed to do something. She couldn't let this rabble rouser get away with harming Mary-Elizabeth. Ruth sat with mouth agape and hands clasping the edge of the table. She'd obviously be of no help.

Leaving all caution behind, Amelia fled after the two. Her patience with Jimmy had run out, and his bullying would cease today.

CHAPTER 12

"*E*nough! This is over!" Titus scrambled out of the heap of men, which now consisted of six brawlers. Some fought for Sherwood, some fought for Hooper, while some... Some men just enjoyed a good excuse to throw a punch and wallow on the floor like uncivilized cavemen.

Standing, Titus brushed the wrinkles out of his suit pants, then grabbed a man in each hand. After yanking them aside, he grabbed two more and tugged until they moved. "I said, *enough*! Cease this barbarianism at once!"

Hooper and Sherwood released their holds on each other and stood, hair disheveled, cheeks flaming, nostrils flaring.

Titus folded his arms across his middle, then shoved his shoulders back. Glaring at both men while attempting to ignore the rumble of voices all around him from the guests who seemed to enjoy the break in civility, he grunted. "Grown men of your standing should never behave like this, especially in the presence of women and children. I'd have expected more from men with your reputations." He scanned all six of them. Only Hooper and one other seemed remorseful for the ruckus they'd caused.

"*Mr.* Overton—"

"No, I will not hear an excuse." He held up his hand and halted Sherwood's words. "You and your family will leave Point Clear today. I've tried to be gracious, but you're no longer welcome at the Grand."

"You have no authority to send us away. The matter's already been settled. The storm prevents us from leaving." Sherwood arched his left eyebrow and grinned.

"By sea, maybe. Nothing prohibits your departure by land."

"That will take too long, Overton!"

"I'm sorry, but it has to be this way." Titus turned to Felix, who had become one of his favorite employees. "See to it Mr. Sherwood and his family are loaded up on the coach and on their way to Bay Minette before noon."

Focusing his gaze on Sherwood, he stifled the grin he wanted to display. He shouldn't take pleasure in publicly shaming a man. "Collect your family and belongings, Mr. Sherwood."

When a hand clutched his forearm, Titus stiffened, prepared to defend himself and his quest.

"Sir, please don't send us away." A woman at least a foot shorter than him peeked up at him from beneath a black feather-adorned hat. "My husband and my son will no longer misbehave. I can guarantee you. I see no reason why my daughters and I should be penalized for their behavior." She turned an icy gaze on Sherwood and scowled at him.

Sherwood's shoulders slumped, and for the first time since Titus had made his acquaintance, he seemed to cower. So...Mrs. Sherwood was actually the one in charge.

"Dear—"

"No, Lloyd. No more. You've tarnished my reputation for the last time. You can return home with Jimmy, but if Mr. Overton will allow me and the girls to stay, we'd like that. That will give the two of you time to decide what's most important to you—our family and the status and wealth that comes with it, or your quest to intimidate everyone you meet. My father did not build our empire so you could tear it down. I suggest you decide carefully."

Mrs. Sherwood glanced up at Titus again.

He couldn't deny her based off the poor choices her husband and son had made. "Mrs. Sherwood, you and your daughters are welcome to stay until your reserved time ends. However, I have to caution you that you won't have an escort to accompany you home to..."

"Atlanta. And that's fine. I'm quite accustomed to managing on my own."

Titus nodded. "Very well."

"Thank you." Mrs. Sherwood removed her hand from Titus's arm, then pivoted away without another glance at her husband.

"Felix, carry out my orders, please."

"You'll regret this, Overton."

"I doubt that." Titus straightened his coat as Felix removed Sherwood from the room and the guests disbanded.

Hooper grabbed Titus's shoulder. "My family. Where are they? Did you see them leave?"

"No, sir. I didn't. Perhaps they returned to your quarters during the unruliness?"

Releasing his arm, Hooper called to anyone within hearing range. "Has anyone seen my wife and daughters? Anyone?"

A pang of fear pierced Titus's chest. Where was Amelia? She'd been here at the table with the Hoopers.

"They ran out that way." A waiter pointed out the side door which led to the croquet lawn. "They went after the photographer who chased Mr. Sherwood's son."

Titus ran his hands through his hair. "And you didn't think to go after them to make sure everyone was safe?"

Hooper bolted toward the door.

Titus shook his head at the waiter. "We'll continue this conversation later."

Following Hooper, he prayed he'd find everyone safe—especially Amelia.

~

"Jimmy! You don't want to do this." Amelia halted a few feet from the boy who held Mary-Elizabeth in his grasp beneath the cluster of trees.

"Stay there! Don't tell me what I want. I want her. And I'll have her."

"No, you'll never have me!" Mary-Elizabeth held onto Jimmy's forearms and attempted to twist out of his grip.

"I already do!" He cackled.

Amelia stepped closer to the troubled lad, her heart breaking over his distress. Why did he feel the urge to take things that didn't belong to him? And now a young woman?

With her hands held out in front of her, she took another step toward him. "Jimmy, what you are doing is far worse than taking my camera or setting fire to the storage shed. This is kidnapping. You'll go to jail. Sheriff Franklin won't see you as a child. He'll see you as a grown man who harmed another person. Please let her go!"

Where were the others? Where was Titus? Was he still in the dining hall with Mr. Sherwood and Mr.

Hooper as they wrestled on the floor? Wasn't anyone coming to rescue Mary-Elizabeth?

"I won't go to jail. My father—"

"Your father is the laughingstock of society!" Mary-Elizabeth screamed at him while continuing to twist free.

Jimmy slipped one of his arms around her neck. "Take it back! Don't say that about my father."

Despite gagging for her next breath, Mary-Elizabeth twisted once more, then kicked backward, landing a blow to Jimmy's right shin.

When he yelped, Amelia sprang forward with all her strength and tackled Jimmy to the ground, forcing him to release his hold on Mary-Elizabeth.

Despite his squirming beneath her and his squeals like a stuck pig, she pressed her knees into his back. Glancing to her right, her gaze landed on Mary-Elizabeth where she sat on the ground weeping. "Are you hurt?"

Swiping tears from her rosy cheeks, she shook her head. "No, I don't think so. Thank you."

"No need to thank me. You saved yourself." Amelia winked at her.

"Amelia? What is...what happ..." Titus called from over her left shoulder.

She turned her head toward him and burst into laughter at the sight of him.

With hair tousled, bruising all around his eyes, and

a trickle of blood coming from his left cheek, he was probably the most handsome man she'd ever seen.

No, not probably.

Definitely.

"I made an arrest." She smiled. "Now if you'd be so kind as to attend to my prisoner, I can get up off the ground and attempt to salvage what remains of my dignity."

"Yes, yes, of course." Titus offered her his hand, helped her to her feet, and then yanked Jimmy off the ground.

Amelia turned to aid Mary-Elizabeth, but her family already surrounded her. Brushing grass and sand off her skirt, she heaved a sigh.

This was a day to write about in her diary and maybe even about which to send a letter home to Aunt Patsy and Aunt Polly—one to each of them because they often reminded her they were two separate people each with their own affiliation with her. Maybe she'd leave out the part about her tackling Jimmy lest they think she'd become a barbarian while here.

~

*N*ow that the week's storms had rolled back out to sea and the resort had settled down from the chaos surrounding the Sherwood family, Titus savored the calm that had perched over Point Clear. What he'd once deemed as a complete bore, he now soaked in, letting his body relax beneath the late-July sun.

From his seat at the pavilion at the water's edge, he watched Amelia at work, laughing as she photographed families frolicking in the waters. Her giggle floated on the breeze and invigorated him. The charm which bubbled from deep inside her made every new acquaintance a friend, and she didn't even realize she had that effect on them. That's what made her so lovely.

Their time together yesterday after church and the noon meal beneath the trees reading more from the book of Matthew still lingered in his thoughts. She'd be leaving in four weeks, and he desired only to ask her to stay.

But she had a life in Philadelphia. A future as a successful photographer. He couldn't be so selfish as to ask her to give that up for him.

Besides, his time here would end soon, too, as soon as he found a replacement. If he had to decide today, he'd pick Felix, for he had exhibited great leadership qualities.

With the uncertainty of where his freedom would land him, he couldn't ask Amelia to consider choosing him.

He most certainly could not.

∽

*A*melia stretched her neck from left to right, the crackles at the base of her skull announcing her exhaustion. Sucking in a cleansing breath, she flexed her hands, then gave one last smile to the Hooper family. Even though Mr. Hooper still sported a blackened eye and a bruised lower lip, he'd posed with the grace and elegance of a king for the portrait in front of the bay that his wife and daughters had coerced him into sitting for. These women loved him and now seemed to hold him in an even higher regard than they had before he'd defended them against Sherwood.

"Thank you again, Miss Amelia." Mary-Elizabeth smiled.

Amelia nodded. "Yes, of course. Now I believe I'll find a shady spot at one of the pavilions on the water and see if I can capture some seabirds frolicking before the evening meal."

After she packed her camera away, she hoisted the case off the sand and scurried up the slope to the path which led to the pavilions. Despite her donning of her pink linen blouse and mint-green cotton skirt, the heat had blazed down on her and turned her into a melted puddle. What she wouldn't give right now for a bowl of sweet snow cream. Maybe she should stop at the beverage cart for a glass of water or lemonade before finding a spot at the pavilion.

She halted, case dangling in front of her legs. No, she'd be fine once she got to the shade.

Amelia scanned the pavilions and found one that looked unoccupied from this distance, so she headed toward it.

With only four weeks left in Point Clear, she needed a few more adventures to make her travels memory-worthy. Could she arrange another trip to Fort Morgan before the threat of late-summer storms doused the opportunity? Perhaps a boat ride over to Weeks Bay for a tour of the bog and the habitat there? She'd read about the carnivorous plants that called the bog their home and the colorful birds and butterflies too. They would make excellent subjects for her photography.

She still needed to photograph Titus for the wall in the main building, but he'd given another excuse to her the last time she'd asked. A valid excuse. For the general manager could not display a black eye and busted lip in his portrait.

Still...she'd favor having a portrait of him that way as a keepsake.

Any portrait of him would suffice because in a few short weeks, she'd have nothing but her memories of him when she returned to Philadelphia, except for maybe a few shots she'd captured of him associating with the guests.

Trying to keep her chin held high and her eyes dry, Amelia made her way down the boardwalk to the pavilion.

Her gaze landed on a figure leaning back on the

bench, and a sigh escaped her. She wouldn't find solace at this pavilion.

When the gentleman turned to face her, her breath caught in her throat as a smile commandeered her face.

She'd find something more valuable than solace here today.

"Titus." His name slipped from her lips as he rose and offered her a seat on the bench.

CHAPTER 13

*S*omething felt different about Titus. He'd invited her to join him, yet he wasn't really present with her. Perhaps the silver waves and bird calls had captivated him so much that he felt no need for conversation.

But his silence left a void in Amelia's heart. Her tendency would be to fill the space with words, be they empty or meaningful, just so they wouldn't sit in silence.

Maybe he'd learned something about the calm she hadn't. Maybe words weren't necessary, after all.

Beside her feet, her case sat with her camera inside, begging to capture Titus on film. She'd asked too many times already. She couldn't ask him again.

With her hands folded on her lap, she focused her gaze out on the bay even though her thoughts continued to race about this change in Titus.

He'd been exuberant when he'd shared about his newfound faith. When Mr. Sherwood and Jimmy made a mess of things at the resort, his passion for justice leached out of his pores. And he'd stated on more than one occasion he'd do whatever he must to keep her safe.

Then why the sudden change?

Why this quiet?

Why invite her to join him yet make her feel as though she didn't belong here?

Maybe she should excuse herself under the guise of needing to rest before the evening meal?

Clearing the hesitation from her throat, Amelia sat up straighter on the bench. Not pulling her gaze from the water, she swallowed down the knot which held her voice captive. "Titus—"

"I love you." His voice trembled like a fawn's legs upon standing for the first time.

Had she heard him correctly? Had the breeze changed his words into something she wanted to hear?

As her heart took flight, she licked her parched lips. Had she wanted him to say these words?

"You don't have to say anything. My declaration of love to you isn't cause for action on your part, and it isn't meant to make you feel like a caged bird. I don't expect you to reciprocate in any way. I only needed to tell you how I feel because since I've found God, my heart is changing. It's more malleable. It's open to receiving love again."

Amelia faced him, searching the side of his face while his gaze remained focused on the water. "Again?"

Titus nodded, then shifted to face her. "I was engaged to be married once."

"Oh." Someone else had held his heart? And broken it? How could she?

"Her name was Evelyn. She...died...of malaria." His gaze remained locked on hers, never wavering.

"I'm so sorry." That explained it, for surely, only death could cause someone to leave this man.

"I've spent every day since her death being angry, feeling cheated and lied to. Everyone talks about having a happily ever after, but mine was ripped away from me."

All the moisture left Amelia's mouth and throat. What could she say to comfort him? She'd never known this kind of loss—not even when she'd lost Mama and Pa.

"But when I met God, He showed me that my life was just beginning. That I didn't go to the grave with Evelyn, and that it was fine to live—and love—again."

Amelia arched her right eyebrow as she tilted her head to the left. "So you picked me to love?" Was she the next best thing to Evelyn? The easiest choice for Titus? If that's why he'd declared his love, he could take the declaration back.

He shook his head while twirling the right corner of his mustache between his fingers. "No, no, I'm sorry to have made it sound that way. I'm such a fool. From the moment I saw you on the boardwalk the day you arrived, I've been unable to get you out of my thoughts. I took a liking to you but told myself that was all it could ever be. But as I've said before, you've haunted my every waking thought and my dreams too."

He took her right hand in his left and stroked it with his thumb. "My fear over losing again made me cast all hopes of something between us out to sea. There were —are—too many obstacles in our paths. You're leaving and I'll never see you again. I don't even know where I'll be after the summer ends. So you see, there's no use even considering something between us."

Amelia frowned at Titus. In the same breath, he'd declared his love, then told her they were doomed. "Hmm, sounds as though you've got it all worked out, and you don't need to hear if I have the same affection for you. So why even mention it? Why declare your love for me? Why drag me down into your hopeless pit without first giving me the chance to voice my observation?"

Titus's mouth fell open as he released her hand. Standing, he marched to the railing and looked out to sea. "I simply wanted you to know how absolutely wonderful you are so you'll never doubt it. You need to know how utterly impossible it is for a man not to fall in love with you. But I'd never expect someone like you to accept someone like me, to uproot her whole life without knowing where she may land. I just wouldn't ever be so selfish."

"Why not?"

"Why not what?"

Amelia left her seat on the weathered bench and occupied the spot next to Titus, leaving less than an inch between their arms. Gripping the splintered railing, she let her gaze search the waters for dolphins as she found her words. "Why wouldn't you expect me to accept you, to uproot my life? Why would you think loving me would be selfish? Who am I that you'd think you are somehow not worthy of me?"

Titus turned toward her. His gaze searched her face, penetrated her soul.

If she faced him now, if she admitted to him and to herself that he had awakened her heart, if she declared she loved him...

Was this love? Was it more than infatuation? For whatever this was, if she spoke to him what her heart felt right now, there would be no going back. There would be no moving forward without him by her side. The chances of meeting someone in Philadelphia who might hold a higher place in society than Titus would be snuffed out. Would her aunts even approve of him? Did she care if they did or didn't? Now that he'd awakened her desire for love and she'd seen it wasn't anything to be afraid of, maybe she'd have more success with the gentlemen back home. Maybe her purpose here this summer had been to slough off the bindings around her heart. Maybe—

Amelia pivoted toward Titus so fast that she lost her balance.

With quick hands and strong arms, he stabilized her, keeping his warm hands on her elbows.

How had her hands ended up on his chest? His heart drummed beneath her right hand and sent waves of delight up her arm and straight to her heart. "Why not?"

❧

*D*id Amelia feel his racing heart beneath her hand? Of course she did, for it threatened to leap from his chest and set the sea grass afire.

Titus pulled her closer, although he shouldn't because if she didn't love him, then this closeness would only cause more damage to him—and she'd feel obligated. He never wanted her to feel an obligation to be with him.

"Because I can't give you surety of what the future brings. Because you deserve a fine home with a staff to wait on you and fulfill your every need."

She threw her head back as a snicker erupted from her, sending her hat to the floor and her blonde waves tumbling around her shoulders.

"I'm sincere! You deserve so much more than me. You deserve a man who knows God much better than I do. You—"

"*I* need you to stop trying to run me off like a stray

cat." Amelia slid her hands from his chest, then wrapped them around the back of his neck while imprisoning his gaze. "I need you to trust me and to believe that any decision I make will be made from a sound mind, a mature heart, and will not be made due to coercion or obligation. I know what I want."

The heat exuding from her body penetrated his suit and sent waves and tingles down to his toes. Her heart pounded against his chest. Were they really that close? Should they be that close?

Titus would have checked to see if they had any spectators watching them, but his gaze remained locked on Amelia's sapphire-like eyes. Swallowing against a parched mouth and throat, he shifted his hands to her waist and drew her even closer, if that was possible. "And what is it you want?"

A grin spread from her mouth to her eyes. She gave two squeezes to the back of his neck, then sighed. "You. I want you. Because...I love you too."

Titus didn't give her the chance to take back her words. He captured her mouth with his and savored her response to him. For she did respond. She hungrily received his kiss and gave back a double portion.

Then her hands left his neck, and she wrapped her arms around his waist, pulling him closer. They were like two pieces of a puzzle that had been separated and had finally found each other again. They fit perfectly together.

Titus continued to drink in Amelia's love until she

tugged her mouth from his with labored breathing. She stared up into his eyes with eyes as glassy as the bay, the area around her lips chafed and rosy from his whiskers.

Bringing a gloved finger to her mouth, she traced her bottom lip as a smile made its home there.

If this weren't a Monday, if only it were a Sunday, Titus would summon the minister this very moment and have him pronounce them husband and wife.

Warning flares shot off inside him. He shouldn't be so presumptuous as to assume Amelia would take his hand in marriage after one single kiss. She might have found it repulsive, might now be trying to think of a polite way to excuse herself and reject his affections, as Mary-Elizabeth had rejected Jimmy.

"Do you still mean it, Amelia Harris?"

"I do, Titus Overton. And you?"

"Even more."

Reaching up, Amelia stroked his bottom lip with her thumb. "Did I hurt your mouth? It's still bruised."

Titus captured her hand and squeezed it. "I felt not one single ounce of pain. In fact, your kiss was the balm I needed." Then he retrieved her hat from the floor and handed it to her, only then noticing flowers replaced the feathers that had once adorned it. "You altered your hat?"

She nodded. "I did. It seemed disrespectful to wear the plumes of feathered friends who might possibly be endangered."

"Even more, Miss Harris. I love you even more."

∽

*E*ach day that passed after their declaration endeared Amelia to Titus more and made him reluctant to attend to his duties at the resort. If he'd had no responsibilities, he'd charter a sailboat every day and sail around the bay from sunup to sundown with no one but his love accompanying him.

His duties, however, remained a priority until he found his replacement—which still seemed it would be Felix.

On Friday morning at breakfast, Titus stood at the entrance to the dining hall where he'd stood every day the resort had guests and welcomed the vacationers into the building.

"Morning." Titus nodded at the gentlemen, tipped his hat to the ladies.

Three new families had joined them yesterday when the boat arrived. They'd stay through the end of August.

A dagger pierced his heart at the thought of August's end, when Amelia's time here would conclude and decisions would need to be made. Titus had already decided he would accompany her home to Philadelphia, if she'd allow, and ask her aunts for their blessing in marriage. They could live there until they knew God's path for them.

When someone cleared her throat, Titus pulled his

attention back to his station, then smiled as his gaze landed on Amelia.

"You must've been lost in thought, for I said good morning to you three times." A giggle floated from her mouth.

"Indeed. Lost in thoughts of you. Good morning, my dear."

"Good morning. If you have no pressing business to attend to after breakfast, I had an idea for an outing that would require a gentleman's presence."

Titus's eyebrows lifted high on his forehead as interest in her plan sparked in his heart. Pulling her out of the doorway and onto the grass beside the building so guests could enter for breakfast, he focused all his attention on her. "Do tell me your idea."

As she clasped her hands in front of her, she raised her shoulders up to her chin and smiled again. "There's a bog on Weeks Bay that's home to rare pitcher plants, birds I've never seen in Philadelphia, and beautiful butterflies. I'd love to take a few of the children there today so we can capture photographs of these things. Would you consider escorting us?"

She needn't ask him twice. Of course he would. He'd leave Felix in charge of the resort for the day and see how he managed.

"I've been trying to come up with a way to spend some time with you away from here, and this is what I came up with."

"So you don't really care about photographing the

plants and animals?" He winked at her while twirling his mustache.

She returned his wink, tugging on her left earlobe and smiling once again. "Oh, I do. I do. Most assuredly. I can't imagine returning home without having captured them." When her smile faded into a frown and a cavern traced its way across her brow, she dipped her head.

Titus cupped her chin and pulled it upward until her gaze met his. "Amelia?"

She swatted his concern away with her hand. "Pay no mind to me. Summer's end keeps haunting me."

"I have a suggestion for how we can rectify that problem."

"You do?" She blinked away the mist that filled her eyes.

"I do. But I won't share it with you just yet. Run along and eat until you're stuffed while I arrange for a boat and for someone to manage things while I'm gone."

As her face brightened, she nodded. "Will do!"

And with that, she pivoted and disappeared into the dining hall.

Titus headed to his office to make arrangements for a day Amelia wouldn't soon forget.

CHAPTER 14

*T*oday held so much perfection, Amelia couldn't believe this wasn't heaven. The white-speckled carnivorous plants that danced with perfection in the breeze, the birds decorated with patterns she'd never seen, the wood ducks floating on the Fish River as though they hadn't a care in the world —all these creatures didn't seem to belong here. Surely, heaven was this magnificent.

Amelia released a gentle moan. To be here in the boat with Titus, Mae, Goldie, and Willis made this the best day she'd had since stepping off the *Baldwin* almost two months ago. That wide-eyed young woman had indeed not known what the Lord had in store for her in Point Clear, how her life would change. While she'd had regrets about coming after she'd first arrived, feared feeling alone the whole summer, now she regretted only that she'd leave this place soon.

Amelia adjusted her hat to shade her face from the sun which beamed overhead, shoving her dismay deep within her. She wouldn't let anything ruin this day.

Peering into the viewfinder of her Brownie again, she focused on a patch of red-and-purple pitcher plants beyond Titus, who sat at the back of the sailboat steering it. Then she shifted her focus to him and held the button down, capturing him, as majestic as any Greek statue.

Firm chin, regal nose, sturdy neck, sun-kissed hair like the sand—he was everything.

She advanced the film, then pressed the button again as his gaze shifted to her and a smile peeked out from underneath his mustache.

She wasn't as clever as she'd thought. He'd known she was capturing him. Capturing his image forever, as he'd captured her heart.

When he joined her on the bench at the front of the boat, she let her camera dangle around her neck as she clasped her seat and forced herself not to wrap her arms around this man.

After he scooted next to her, he pressed his upper arm against hers. "Mae, might I beg a favor of you?"

Mae pulled her attention from the manatee indulging in the vegetation at the water's edge. "Yes, sir. Of course."

Titus held his hand out toward Amelia's camera, then raised his eyebrows in a request that didn't need voicing.

She lifted her strap off her neck and handed the camera to him. What did he want with it?

Passing it to Mae, he leaned against Amelia again, sending more heat through her than the sun had. "Please capture Miss Harris and myself in several photographs."

Goldie giggled, then Mae did the same. They had to sense the love that blossomed between their chaperones.

For it blossomed, indeed.

Neither one could deny it. Amelia didn't want to.

By the time Titus pulled the boat up to the board-walk, Amelia had used every bit of her one-hundred-exposure roll of film. A little more than half the photographs had captured nature, but the rest contained memories of them together. The perfect day couldn't get any more perfect than this.

But as Titus twirled Amelia around the dance floor after dinner, his left hand encircling her waist and his right hand cupping her left, Amelia's heart soared to new heights. While there were at least twenty other couples on the floor with them, her focus remained on Titus, who seemed to be living life for the first time tonight.

Had he ever danced with Evelyn like this? He must have because he was no novice. His expertise spoke of much time paired with a woman in dance. Whoever it had been, Amelia owed her many thanks, because as they stepped out the three-fourths rhythm to *Over the*

Waves, her pink skirt swishing as it touched his suit pants, Titus made her feel like a princess. Around and around they twirled, his hand pulling her even closer to him. He kept his gaze locked with hers until he drew her against him, resting his lips on her left ear.

"Marry me, Amelia Harris?"

The tingle that came from drinking mint tea raced through Amelia's body. The coolness of the mint. The heat of the tea. Shivers of delight. Shocks like lightning.

Amelia pressed her lips against his left ear. "Yes, my love. Yes!"

Titus released a chuckle that sent more ripples of enchantment through her. Would their life together be filled with laughter and love neither had felt before?

Most assuredly, it would be.

For now until forever.

Two pops followed by panicked screams halted their feet and nearly stopped Amelia's heart.

Before she had time to focus her gaze on the happenings around her, Titus shoved her to the floor. "Get underneath the table and hide beneath the tablecloth."

She clung to his forearms. "What? I don't—"

He shoved her under the table, causing the tablecloth to tug toward her and knives and forks to tumble to the floor with a clank. "Do not come out until I come get you."

More pops followed by more screams sent Amelia scrambling beneath the table.

Gunfire.

A shooter had invaded their time of glee. And now her dear love—her first love—had spared her, yet placed himself in harm's way to save his guests.

Lifting the fabric, she scooted toward the edge of the round table, then halted, fear trembling through her hands. Titus had told her to stay. If she crawled out and suffered at the hands of this assailant, Titus might not forgive her—or worse, might not forgive himself, especially if she succumbed to any injuries.

Amelia scurried to the center of the table, letting the tablecloth slip from her grasp, and settled on the floor as the darkness engulfed her.

More pops.

More screams.

More footsteps scrambling away.

Amelia clasped her hands over her ears and tried to drown out the chaos. Tried to snuff out the accusations in her head that screamed how weak and ineffective she was.

No, she wasn't cowardly at all. If she was going to fulfill her calling, she needed to remain safe and let Titus fight for her.

Her strength came from admitting her insufficiency in this moment—and from trusting God to protect the man she loved.

As quickly as the chaos began, it ended.

No more shots from the gun.

No more screams.

Titus would come for her at any moment.

Yet minutes passed and he never came.

~

*T*itus wiped the blood from his hands onto the linen napkin he retrieved from the table at the kitchen doorway. "Felix, send two men for the sheriff and the undertaker. Send some staff into the crowd to inquire if we have a doctor with us. I believe one of the new guests is one. Send someone for the nurse at the infirmary. I don't believe she's in the dining hall tonight."

"Yes, sir. What of..." Felix lowered his gaze to the floor.

Titus stared at the dead man who lay at their feet, the man whose blood had stained his hands moments before. "Cover him with one of the tablecloths until the undertaker arrives. I don't want a single guest to lay eyes on this tragedy."

"Of course, sir."

He locked gazes with Felix. "I'll be in the storage room with the board of directors and this man's accomplices trying to understand why this happened." He shook his head while attempting to swallow down the fury which burned inside him. Why would this band of men have come into their festivities and fired upon these innocent people? What had any of them done to deserve such a despicable act?

Titus pivoted away from Felix, biting his tongue and resisting the urge to seek revenge.

The Lord will fight for you and for these people. He will vindicate this wrong.

Titus must trust that God would take care of this.

As he reached the storage room where the board of directors had taken the men into custody, he halted as his thoughts returned to the moments before the attack.

Amelia!

Was she still seeking shelter beneath the table as he'd asked? Had she followed his orders, or had she attempted to take on the role of protector that she usually did?

Pivoting, he stared into the dimly lit room scattered with too many tables. Where had they been dancing when the aggressors barged into their revelry?

Titus lifted the fabric on the first table he came to.

No Amelia.

Table after table, he raised the tablecloths, searched beneath them but didn't find her. Titus turned, then wheeled about again, running his hands through his hair. "Amelia! Amelia!" He spun around again. "Amelia Harris, where are you?"

Out of the corner of his right eye, a slow movement captured his attention, coming from underneath a table one row over from the dancefloor on which he stood.

With the tablecloth lifted, Amelia crawled from beneath the table.

Titus wasted not a second to get to her, his shoes

sliding on the polished heart pine floor. "Amelia! Are you unscathed?" He clasped her upper arms and held her away from him to inspect her.

"I am. I am, Titus." She clasped the back of his forearms. "Are you hurt? What happened?"

He released her arms and took her hands in his. "I'm unharmed. Men came in with guns and began shooting."

"Wh-why? Who would do such a thing?"

Titus shook his head. He didn't have an answer for Amelia.

Yet.

But he would after he interrogated the men alongside the board members who'd dined with them tonight.

"I'll let you know when I know. We're waiting on the sheriff, but while we do, I'll be seeking answers from the men. You can stay here at a table...or perhaps go outside with the other guests. Anywhere but here. There may be some children who need comforting in a way only you can do."

"I want to stay with you."

Titus shook his head again as he locked his gaze on hers. Even in the dimness, the fear in her eyes infiltrated him and made him want to leave the questioning of these men to the board so he could hold her until her fears subsided.

"You should be spared what may occur as we perform our investigation. Now, I must go. I'll find you later." He didn't give her time to argue. Spinning away from her, he marched to the storage room, yanked the door open, and slammed it behind him.

Three men sat on the floor, leaning against the shelving, hands behind their backs. Their black bandannas hung around their necks and rested on their chests, no longer covering their faces. Each man, with dark hair and shifty eyes, wore black trousers and black coats, little distinguishing one from the other.

"What do you have to say for yourselves?" He glared at each one. Then, turning his focus to the board members standing before him—first Jones, then Matthews, then Baker—he raised his right eyebrow and shrugged. "Have they explained the meaning of this?"

Matthews released a groan as he swiped sweat from his plump face. "They said only that Sherwood had arranged for them to join him here so they could conspire against those who resisted the change Governor Jelks is instituting."

Titus returned his gaze to the men, each studying him with what felt like distain. What had he done to them? "Sherwood had planned to use the resort to start some kind of revolution against people who wanted to help the poor and the minorities? You brought weapons here to harm innocent people?"

The man on the far left wiggled his feet as he fought against the ropes which bound his hands. "No, we came for you." He sneered.

The man in the middle scowled at him. "You had

him removed from the resort. Word didn't come to us because we were on the boat here. When we arrived and found out he wasn't here and why—"

"We knew you needed to be held accountable," the man on the right added. "You and the owner, Reuben Kroyer. You're responsible for our wasted trip here and for our plans being delayed."

Titus glanced at the board members, focusing on Jones. "Where's Kroyer? Has anyone made sure he's unharmed?"

The men on the floor hooted.

Titus darted his gaze at them, then back to Jones.

Jones's shoulders slumped. "They found him in his quarters first before coming to find you."

Heat raced through him. His throat squeezed shut. His stomach churned and threatened to spew its contents at his feet. "What are you saying?"

"One of them killed him."

Titus swung around to face the men again. "Which one of you has done this horrible thing? Reuben Kroyer fought to allow Sherwood to stay. He had nothing to do with his expulsion. You killed an innocent man!"

While Titus had only tolerated Kroyer, he could not bear knowing he had died because of Titus's need to see Sherwood removed. His blood was on his hands. How would he ever forgive himself? How would God? Even Amelia would blame him for the incident.

Titus removed his handkerchief from his pocket and swiped the sweat from his face. Releasing a heavy sigh, he turned back to the board members. "Stay with these criminals until the deputies arrive. Don't let them devise an escape plan." He turned the knob and yanked the door open. Then he halted and spun back around. "Who killed their leader?"

Baker smirked. "Hooper. Apparently, after his skirmish with Sherwood and what his daughter Mary-Elizabeth endured with Jimmy, he decided to keep his weapon with him at all times. When the disruption broke out, he went into action. Their leader had his gun aimed at you, so Hooper took him out."

Titus returned his handkerchief to his pocket as a smile graced his face. But a smile couldn't convey the gratitude that swept through him like a tidal wave. He stood here unscathed because Hooper had been on guard against danger. He owed him his very life. He would never be able to repay him for his gallantry, but he would sure try.

After exiting the room, he searched until he found Amelia where he thought she'd be—on the lawn with children surrounding her, patting them on the tops of their heads and rubbing their shoulders.

God had sent him a woman who was grander than any angel in heaven. A blessed man he was indeed.

Peace settled in his heart. Amelia wouldn't hold him responsible for Kroyer's death. She'd only argue that Titus had been wrong for assuming his own culpability in the situation. She'd remind him of grace. Grace that he'd have a lifetime to explore with her by his side.

EPILOGUE

Five months later

The enchantment of December on Mobile Bay still sent tingles to Amelia's toes every morning. Or was it the fact that she awoke in the owner's quarters on the western side of the resort facing the sparkling waters with Titus lying beside her?

Yes, that was it.

While avoiding a snow-filled Christmas this year did bring delight to Amelia's soul, waking daily as Mrs. Amelia Overton, Titus's wife, brought pink to her cheeks and oxygen to every cell in her body.

Although they'd been married since the Sunday following the shooting—two days after Titus had asked her to become his wife there on the dance floor—time with him remained fresh and new every second.

Even though he'd inherited the resort from Reuben

Kroyer, which had surprised everyone, including the board of directors, Titus made her his priority—after God, of course.

Amelia lifted the steaming mug of hot chocolate to her lips beneath the pavilion where Titus had declared his love for her. At this very spot, she'd declared her love for him too. Each morning after Titus met with Felix, his new general manager, to ensure the resort ran as smoothly as a sailboat slipping through the bay, he joined her here for their dolphin watch. Sometimes the enchanting mammals greeted them ten feet from the pavilion. Sometimes they remained beyond reach but still in sight.

Amelia couldn't believe that she had captured several photographs of the dolphins as they'd come up for air. Her life here held more blessing than she'd ever felt she deserved. Even Aunt Polly and Aunt Patsy had nothing contrary to say when they'd visited during the fall after the storms left the area. How could they have had anything against the man she'd chosen and the life they now lived? It was as perfect as one's life could ever be.

"Good morning, my love. Do you have room for a gentleman caller?"

Amelia set her mug beside her, then patted the bench at her right. "For you? Always. How are things with the resort and the guests this morning?"

Titus lowered himself beside her, his body bringing her warmth and comfort even though the air was neither crisp nor frigid, like her family endured back home. Titus's presence always warmed her. "All's well with the resort. Are you ready for our adventure?"

She nodded. "I am, indeed. Who wouldn't look forward to the annual Christmas Bird Count?"

Titus tapped her nose with his right forefinger, then kissed her cheek. "My lovely wife, I can without much doubt guarantee you that you are the only woman here at the Grand with any interest in the National Audubon Society's commitment to ensure the security of migratory birds."

She shrugged. "Perhaps, but you know I'm not like the average woman. If I can help count the terns, egrets, herons, and our beloved gulls while also capturing images of them with my camera and perhaps sneaking a few memories of my handsome husband when he's not aware, my heart will ever be so happy. And even more happy if the bird count excuses me from the obligatory tea and gossip session with the wealthy guests' wives and their daughters."

Titus pointed out to the bay as a pod of dolphins surfaced, then returned to the depths of the water.

Amelia clapped while allowing a giggle to fill the morning air around them.

"Any regrets?"

She faced Titus, clasping her hands on her lap. "Regrets?"

His eyes still held the glassy bay in them, mirroring

the spirit of freedom he'd found at this very pavilion. "About marrying me? Agreeing to stay here?"

She shook her head while taking his left hand into her right. Bringing it to her lips, she pressed a kiss onto his skin, his cologne mixing with the sea breeze and lighting a fire in her belly. "Never. No regrets ever. You?"

He pulled her into an embrace. "Only that we have somewhere to be this morning. For if we could, I would whisk you away on a sailboat and sail to the middle of the bay where we could remain in each other's embrace the full day, no interruptions, no need for society's rules of etiquette. Just our two hearts exploring the true depths of our love."

Amelia released a moan as Titus captured her lips with his. "Sounds delightful," she whispered between pecks. "Perhaps tomorrow?" As she wrapped her arms around his waist and drew him closer, she melted against him.

"Yes, tomorrow. We'll always have tomorrow."

The End

Did you enjoy this book? We hope so!
**Would you take a quick minute to leave a review
where you purchased the book?**
It doesn't have to be long. Just a sentence or two telling
what you liked about the story!

Receive a FREE ebook and get updates when new Wild
Heart books release: https://wildheartbooks.org/
newsletter

Don't miss the next book in Romance at the Gilded Age Resorts Series!

A *Summer at Thousand Island House*
By Susan G. Mathis

Chapter 1

THOUSAND ISLAND HOUSE
ALEXANDRIA BAY, NY
SUMMER, 1885

Addison Bell breathed a quick prayer as she grasped the door handle of the Thousand Island House's recreation pavilion. "Please, Lord, may this summer change my life."

She froze, a tiny tremble of her jaw betraying her resolve to be strong. What would the future hold for her at such an opulent place? Such a foreign establishment? A three-story building dedicated to nothing but recreation?

For her, a simple farm girl and one-room schoolhouse teacher from Watertown Center, this seemed unconventional—eccentric, even. Yet now, here she was, thirty miles away, at the most celebrated hotel in Alexandria Bay, perhaps in all the Thousand Islands— late for work on her first day.

Before she had the chance to pull herself from her ponderings and enter the pavilion, someone pushed open the door she still held, sending her flying onto her backside, skirts flapping in the breeze. Her arms and legs flailed like an octopus out of water. Her carpetbag went flying too. Right into the path of a stalwart gentleman. Her gaze traveled from his toes to his nose. A naval officer, of all people.

The man tripped over her bag but somehow kept his balance. Then he turned to her with a furrowed brow as he reached for her hand, concern marring his handsome face. "Are you all right, miss?"

"Yes, thank you, sir. I'm sorry I tripped you up." A nervous giggle slipped out as she accepted his hand, her cheeks burning at the thought of her buffoonery.

The officer tugged her to her feet, and she furiously smoothed her skirts. Her well-worn straw hat flopped to one side, dangling precariously over one eye. She righted it as best she could, ignoring the pins poking into her scalp. She must look affright.

"I am the one who must apologize for opening the door and sending you aloft." He paused for a moment and tipped his hat. "Lieutenant Maxwell Worthington of the US Navy." He clicked his heels before snapping a quick nod her way. "At your service, miss."

Addi curtsied low and sucked in a steadying breath. Then she pasted on a smile. "Pleased to meet you, Lieutenant, but I must be on my way. I'm late as it is."

"Hurry then, and farewell for now." Lieutenant Worthington picked up her bag and handed it to her.

"Thank you, sir. Good day to you."

Addi regathered her nerve and turned to enter the pavilion. A man stood before her, his title of manager boldly proclaimed on his name tag.

He snapped a concerned glance at the retreating lieutenant and then at her. "Servants should enter at the back, miss. I'll excuse the mishap this once. Aye, both mishaps."

Addi blinked. A hint of Irish floated on the man's words, making them sound like a melody to a faraway tune, even as he scolded her. In public.

"Mr....Mr. Donovan?"

Her words squeaked out as if she were a tiny child. She swallowed her angst, straightening her shoulders to regain some semblance of professionalism.

The man nodded, an almost imperceptible smirk appearing, then fading fast. "Aye, one and the same. You're late. Let's get you settled."

Addi's nerves got the better of her, and her tongue took flight. "I'm sorry I'm tardy, sir. The horse threw a shoe on the way here, and the wagon went into the ditch, and Mr. Stevens didn't know what to do, but then a farmer helped us out, but—"

Mr. Donovan held up his hand to stop her chattering but cast her a kind smile. He took the carpetbag from her and motioned for her to enter the pavilion. "It's all right, miss. This is your day to settle in and prepare for the rest of the summer. You've no children waiting."

"Thank goodness." Addi sighed loudly, adjusting

her teetering hat.

Once inside, Mr. Donovan paused in the foyer and tipped his head, assessing her from her still-teetering hat to her scuffed boots. "Aye, this is the Thousand Island House recreation pavilion, where you will spend the next several months caring for our patrons' children. I must say, your recommendation was quite glowing, especially from my crotchety old friend, Alvin Sanderson. But I didn't expect someone so young to be so accomplished, and from Watertown Center?"

"I'm twenty-four, sir. I've taught up to eighteen children concurrently for the past five years. All ages. All temperaments. And I have to tell you that some of those students, especially the older ones, gave me great consternation. But I overcame their podsnappery with determination and grit." Addi stood as tall as her small frame would rise and lifted her chin.

Mr. Donovan chuckled, wiping the mirth away with the sweep of his hand. "Your enthusiasm is commendable, miss, but quite unnecessary. The former nursery teacher in your position, Mrs. Randolph, barely got off her perch 'cept when it was a matter of life and death. Nevertheless, the parents and children appreciated her grandmotherly ways."

Addi harrumphed, and a small snicker escaped her lips. "I, sir, am not a grandmother, and I believe children are to be given all the fullness of experiences available. Music. Dance. Sports. Nature. Games. Play. And a good dose of God."

"Blathers! You misunderstand. We didn't hire you to teach school. You'll be caring for four-to-seven-year-olds. Mere babes out of diapers." Mr. Donovan sucked in a breath.

"Oh, I don't plan to drill them in the three R's." Addi shook her head. "I simply want to expose them to a wealth of experiences while they're under my care."

Brow knotted, he chewed on his full bottom lip as he studied her—and she him. A generous dollop of Morgan's pomade had to be keeping his curly dark hair in place, else his abundant locks would cover his strong forehead. A full head taller than herself, the man possessed a square chin and high cheekbones that reminded her of royalty, yet his demeanor cast a welcoming, friendly air, even when he frowned.

She stood her ground but turned her attention to the pavilion signs just beyond them—Game Room, Billiard Room, Bowling Alley, Children's Nursery, Men's and Women's Bathing Room, Swimming Pool, and Dancing Pavilion. The choices made her head swim. How could one choose from such lavish entertainments?

Mr. Donovan must have seen her dismay, for he began a tour without addressing her prior comment. "This recreation facility is exclusively for our hotel patrons, though some esteemed visitors not staying at the hotel still come here now and then. As you can see, we have the most modern facilities for entertaining those on summer holiday. Upstairs are various game rooms, mostly for men, which you do not need to see. There are also a grill and garden roof where we host afternoon teas. And more." He patted the nearby desk then pointed beyond it to a tiny room. "This is the reception desk, and that's my office, should you ever need to find me, though I'm often about serving our clients or solving problems." He waved a hand, signaling the end of the brief tour. "This way to the children's nursery, miss."

Mr. Donovan led her down a long hallway. Near the end, he opened the door to a large classroom. "I must admit that your high-minded notions on childcare surprise me. The hotel provides abundant means of children entertaining themselves. Tin toys. Puzzles. Books. And this large room with an ensuite water closet. As far as your duties, you are required only to keep the children safe and quiet."

"Dear me." Addi moaned, curling her hand beneath her chin. "I don't intent to be a jail warden or a prison guard. And I do not adhere to the motto, 'children are to be seen and not heard.' I believe youngsters are like beautiful flowers that are to be nurtured and watered and allowed to blossom and grow into the creatures of beauty God intended them to be. I cannot abide stifling their innate curiosity to learn and grow. I must reinforce it."

Mr. Donovan took a step back, slapping his chest in mock shock. "Blathers! I've hired a radical! Still, you know children better than I, so I will concede to your plans."

"Please, sir. I am not a radical, nor do I mean to impute your idea of childcare, merely to enhance the summer experiences for these little ones." Addi curtsied, humbling herself before her employer.

He chuckled and set her bag on a nearby table. "I understand, but if you deem it necessary to employ your unique ideas, you must get permission from each of the parents to undertake such modern methods. I fear they will view you as merely a babysitter, not a teacher extraordinaire."

"I will, sir. Thank you, sir." Addi clapped her hands, joyful that she'd won the first battle.

She'd won, but surely, from the pluck she'd observed in this Irish manager, there'd be more skirmishes in the days to come.

Liam Donovan shook his head at the strange and lovely lass he'd hired and left in the nursery. Aye, her tongue took to chattering faster than a house-wren's song, but her excitement for teaching children was unmistakable and quite refreshing. Old Mr. Sanderson hadn't warned him of that. Nor of how beautiful she was, with her rich chocolate-brown hair, big, bright eyes warm as melted chocolate, and captivating smile. Blathers! That smile nearly made him go weak at the knees. Then, when she prattled on about her modern methods, it took everything in him not to fawn over her. Yet, as manager of the hotel's recreation pavilion, he had to keep his wits about him.

"Get a hold of yourself, Liam!"

He stopped cold in his tracks upon hearing his own voice.

"Did you say something, sir?" Melvin Olson stared at him with veiled amusement.

A year ago, the recreation leader for their older children and former baseball star had shattered his arm, forever ending his promising career in the sport. Now, he faithfully occupied the eight-to-fourteen-year-old children while their parents enjoyed a life of leisure.

Liam shrugged, raising his palms to the ceiling, then quickly shoving them into his pockets. "Nothing, Mel. Have you any troublemakers in your group of late?"

Melvin popped his gum. "None I can't control. Five silly girls who only want to gossip and talk about boys, and six rambunctious boys who are happy to try to outwit or outrun one another. Easy as batting five hundred."

The lad always referred to baseball, but he was good with kids, and that was what mattered. "Have you enough to keep them busy?"

Snap. "Always. The House provides plenty. Thanks for scheduling them for bowling and swimming once a week. Those'll be the highlight of their time here, without a doubt." Melvin smacked his gum as if he were punctuating his sentence. "Did the nursery teacher arrive?"

"Yes. She's in her room getting settled. I'll introduce her later."

"Fair enough. Better get back to those rascals. Thanks, sir."

Melvin took his leave with another annoying pop, snap, and crack of his gum. The lad was never without his Adams New York chewing gum. Worse than a smoker.

The habit irritated Liam to distraction. Not only was it uncouth and distracting, but it was also a bad habit to model to children. Moreover, a Thousand Island House employee needed to maintain the utmost decorum. Yes, he'd have to talk to him about it—sooner rather than later. Still, habits die hard, and he couldn't afford to offend Melvin and be without a worker right now.

As Liam returned to his desk, Miss Bell's pretty face swept back into his thoughts. Was she as bubbly and vivacious as she appeared, or was it just nerves? His Tina had been like that at first, too, but she gradually withdrew until she'd broken his heart with a rather cold rejection of his marriage proposal. Then, she'd agreed to marry him after all but only days later, left him for his best friend. Aye, well...

After addressing several management situations around the pavilion, Liam decided to check on his newest employee and get her settled in the women's dormitory. He knocked on the classroom door and entered, finding the kitchen maid, Gert, delivering a tray.

"I was told you had six children, plus yourself. Now look at the food that will go to waste." Gert's tone was icy. Harsh, even.

Liam cleared his throat to announce his arrival. "My oversight, miss. I should've sent word the children wouldn't be present today. That wasn't Miss Bell's responsibility. She just arrived an hour ago."

Gert's pudgy face turned red as a ripe tomato, and her tone became syrupy sweet. As it always did when she spoke to him and batted the lashes of her bulgy eyes. It made his stomach clench every time. "Oh, Mr. Donovan. I didn't hear you enter. It's all right. We can add the jam sandwiches to our staff luncheon." She set a wrapped sandwich on the table and glared at Miss Bell. "I'd better get back to the kitchen and help prepare the noon meal. You be certain to let me know in time from here on out."

Miss Bell nodded, a sweet smile begging pardon. Why did Gert have to be so rude?

He smiled as the kitchen maid waddled out the door, smelling of bacon grease and raw chicken. When the door clicked shut, he shrugged. "Sorry about the misunderstanding with the maid. As you've heard, lunch will be delivered to you every day at noon with a snack you can set aside for the afternoon. How do you find your classroom? Do you need anything?"

Miss Bell grinned widely. "This room is well-equipped with the newest books and toys. Thank you. But...I wondered if I might procure a terrarium."

"A what?"

The lovely lass giggled, sounding like melodic wind chimes. "A terrarium. A large glass bowl I can use to arrange plants and moss and bugs and worms and maybe even a frog or two for scientific observation and for the children's enjoyment. It's the latest thing for helping children learn about God's creation."

Liam chuckled at the unconventional request. "You're a rather bricky woman, Miss Bell."

Her brows furrowed, her doe eyes sparking confusion. "Bricky?"

Liam clicked his tongue. "Tenacious. Strong. Like a brick wall. It's meant to be a compliment. Few women would undertake a bug-infested, moss-soaked, frog-hopping science experiment."

Miss Bell waved a hand, her eyes dancing with amusement. "I'm a farmer's daughter. None of that shatters my feminine world."

"Very well, miss. I shall see what I can procure. For now, I'll escort you to the women's dormitory. Then you can familiarize yourself with the hotel and grounds and be ready for the morn." He handed her the sandwich Gert left behind. "Your lunch."

"Thank you, sir. I'd like to be well accustomed to my surroundings before the children come." Miss Bell accepted the sandwich and curtsied.

Liam picked up her carpetbag and led her outside

through the back entrance. "Staff uses this door only. You will care for six children—and sometimes more— for most of the summer. You will lead the children through this entrance as well. You may use this back lawn for play as long as adult patrons are not present. But keep the noise to a minimum, please. And unless there's a special event where children are welcome, you shall not take them to the front of the pavilion and never around or into the hotel itself."

They crossed the small footbridge connecting the pavilion's island to the mainland where the hotel stood.

"Can the children swim? Bowl? Play badminton?"

Liam stopped halfway to the dormitory. "Certainly not, miss. They're babes. They must be older to participate in such activities."

Miss Bell bit her bottom lip but said nothing. Her eyes told a stormy tale of disagreement churning inside. But he'd not open that discussion just now.

Entering the two-story house that was used as the women's dormitory, Liam stopped at the door as the housekeeper joined them. "Good day to you, Mrs. Erving. This is Miss Addison Bell, the nursery worker we've been waiting for."

Mrs. Erving nodded, wiping her wrinkled hands on her apron. Then she swiped her brow with her forearm. "Very good. You'll be bunking with Gert, upstairs, first door on the right." At that, a small groan escaped from Miss Bell, though the housekeeper continued without seeming to notice. "There are two uniforms on the bed, but I daresay they may be too big. Girl, you're skinny as a toothpick! I'll have to find smaller ones."

"Yes, ma'am." Miss Bell curtsied.

Liam sighed. Poor Miss Bell, having to room with prickly Gert. Perhaps he should request a change? No, this was the housekeeper's domain, not his.

Mrs. Erving cast him a scowl and pursed her lips before speaking again. "A few rules. First, no fraternizing with men, either staff or especially not patrons. Either infraction will yield immediate dismissal." Their new nursery worker counted on her fingers as Mrs. Erving provided her list. "Second, keep your room clean and tidy at all times. Third, only women staff are allowed beyond this door." She thrust a fat hand toward the door behind them. "Fourth, no unnecessary noise. Fifth, lights out and all quiet at nine p.m. No exceptions."

Miss Bell closed her fist and clasped her hands together, her mouth pulling tight. She bobbed a curtsy. "Yes, ma'am."

Liam set down her bag and snapped a nod her way. "All right, then, Miss Bell. Get settled and acclimate to your new home. Your shift begins at eight a.m. sharp."

Miss Bell dipped a low curtsy and rewarded him with a bright smile. "Thank you, Mr. Donovan, for this opportunity to serve."

He returned a smile. "Until tomorrow."

Why did he feel he'd be counting the hours until then?

ABOUT THE AUTHOR

Sherri Wilson Johnson is an Inspirational Romance novelist and graphic designer. She lives in Georgia with her husband and their two dogs, and they are empty-nesters. Sherri loves spending time with family, vacationing at the beach, curling up with a good book or working on her current work-in-progress. She dreams of a second home on some beach somewhere some day, where she can plot romantically suspenseful novels all day and night.

Find out more about Sherri on her website: sherriwilsonjohnson.com

Follow Sherri:
  Instagram: instagram.com/swj_thewriter

Facebook: facebook.com/AuthorSherriWilson-Johnson

Goodreads: goodreads.com/author/show/5233294.Sherri_Wilson_Johnson

Bookbub: bookbub.com/authors/sherri-wilson-johnson

TikTok: tiktok.com/@sherriwilsonjohnsonbooks

All links: linktr.ee/sherriwilsonjohnson

ACKNOWLEDGMENTS

To Jesus, first and always: Thank you for giving me another story to tell and a chance to share you with others.

To Dan, thank you for staying on this journey with me and for taking research trips with me.

To all of my family and friends, thank you for your love and support.

To Wild Heart Books, thank you for this opportunity.

If you love historical romance, check out the other Wild Heart books!

Marisol ~ Spanish Rose by Elva Cobb Martin

Escaping to the New World is her only option....Rescuing her will wrap the chains of the Inquisition around his neck.

Marisol Valentin flees Spain after murdering the nobleman who molested her. She ends up for sale on the indentured servants' block at Charles Town harbor —dirty, angry, and with child. Her hopes are shattered, but she must find a refuge for herself and the child she carries. Can this new land offer her the grace, love, and security she craves? Or must she escape again to her only living relative in Cartagena?

Captain Ethan Becket, once a Charles Town minister, now sails the seas as a privateer, grieving his deceased wife. But when he takes captive a ship full of indentured servants, he's intrigued by the woman whose manners seem much more refined than the average Spanish serving girl. Perfect to become governess for his young son. But when he sets out on a quest to find his captured sister, said to be in Cartagena, little does he expect his new Spanish governess to stow away on his ship with her six-month-old son. Yet her offer of help to free his sister is too tempting to pass up. And her beauty, both inside and out, is too attractive for his heart to protect itself against—until he learns she is a wanted murderess.

As their paths intertwine on a journey filled with danger, intrigue, and romance, only love and the grace of God can overcome the past and ignite a new beginning for Marisol and Ethan.

∾

Rocky Mountain Redemption by Lisa J. Flickinger

A Rocky Mountain logging camp may be just the place to find herself.

To escape the devastation caused by the breaking of her wedding engagement, Isabelle Franklin joins her aunt in the Rocky Mountains to feed a camp of lumberjacks cutting on the slopes of Cougar Ridge. If only she could out run the lingering nightmares.

Charles Bailey, camp foreman and Stony Creek's itinerant pastor, develops a reputation to match his new nickname — Preach. However, an inner battle ensues when the details of his rough history threaten to overcome the beliefs of his young faith.

Amid the hazards of camp life, the unlikely friendship growing between the two surprises Isabelle. She's drawn to Preach's brute strength and gentle nature as he leads the ragtag crew toiling for Pollitt's Lumber. But when the ghosts from her past return to haunt her, the choices she will make change the course of her life forever—and that of the man she's come to love.

~

Lone Star Ranger by Renae Brumbaugh Green

Elizabeth Covington will get her man.

And she has just a week to prove her brother isn't the murderer Texas Ranger Rett Smith accuses him of being. She'll show the good-looking lawman he's wrong, even if it means setting out on a risky race across Texas to catch the real killer.

Rett doesn't want to convict an innocent man. But he can't let the Boston beauty sway his senses to set a guilty man free. When Elizabeth follows him on a dangerous trek, the Ranger vows to keep her safe. But who will protect him from the woman whose conviction and courage leave him doubting everything—even his heart?

9 781942 265757